A Visit to Hartington

A Visit
to Hartington

*A short story collection about life in
a small Nebraska town*

◆

Kenny Miller

Writers Club Press
New York San Jose Lincoln Shanghai

A Visit to Hartington
A short story collection about life in a small Nebraska town

All Rights Reserved © 2000 by Kenny R. Miller

Writers Club Press
an imprint of iUniverse.com, Inc.

For information address:
iUniverse.com, Inc.
5220 S 16th, Ste. 200
Lincoln, NE 68512
www.iuniverse.com

ISBN: 0-595-12808-4

Printed in the United States of America

To Mom and Dad.

With very special thanks to Larrie, Nancy, Martha, Willie, and the good people of Hartington, Nebraska.

Hey Little Man

◆

"Have you noticed how quick he is?" the frisky dad asked his wife as he bounced into the kitchen after putting his three-year-old son to bed.

"He has to be quick with you chasing him around the house throwing that football at him," she said as she wiped the kitchen counter dry and turned around to see her husband shadow boxing in front of her.

"It's more than chasing, honey," he said. "He's got good instincts. He's quick and he isn't afraid of the ball when I throw it at him. He catches it. He is going to be a great quarterback. I can see it already."

"Don't you think it is just a bit early for him to go out for football?"

"It's never too early. He is going to be a great athlete. I can just tell."

"That sounds like a father talking."

"A jock father," he said as he gently grabbed his wife's face and gave her a kiss.

"Well jock father, let's call it a day," she said. "If you keep bouncing around down here, he'll want to come down and play."

"I don't think so," he said. "He was pretty tired. Did he seem a little groggy to you tonight?"

"Groggy?" she asked. "No, I didn't think so. Why?"

"He just seemed a little slower than he usually is," the father said.

"That's because as soon as you get home, you start chasing him all over creation with that football."

"He's going to be great and quick because of that my dear wife, just you watch and see."

She shut off the kitchen lights and the two of them headed up the steps for bed. He opened the door to his boy's room and they both peeked inside. Their little blond, blue-eyed boy was sound asleep, one arm clutching a scruffy teddy bear and the other holding the corner of a worn out baby blanket. His dad gently closed the door. Morning and fun with his son would soon come.

"Hey little man," his dad said as he peeked into his boy's room the next morning. His three-year-old son was playing with a green toy farm tractor and a couple of brown plastic cows. The boy sat on the floor in his Gene Autry pajamas, complete with painted guns on the sides.

"Hi Daddy," the boy said as he turned and smiled.

"Ready for some oatmeal? It will help you grow up and become a big strong quarterback."

The boy smiled, gathered up his tractor and plastic cows and looked around for his brown tattered blanket. He pushed himself off of the floor with his right hand. He seemed to teeter a little as he tried to stand and then fell backwards.

"That's too much stuff for a little man to carry," his dad said as he sat down on the floor and brushed his son's blond hair. The boy's forehead felt hot. He watched his son reach out across his body and try to pick up his toy tractor with his right hand. He looked at his left hand, which was closest to the toys. It hung limply at his side.

"Here little man," he said as he put the toy tractor in the boy's left hand, "push it with this hand." He noticed beads of sweat forming on the boy's forehead.

The boy dropped the truck instantly. His left hand and arm fell limp to his side.

"I can do it with this one," the boy said as he smiled at his dad and reached over with his right hand.

"No, push it with this hand."

He took his handkerchief from his pocket and wiped the boy's forehead and placed the back of his hand on the boy's brow. He had a fever, a very high fever. The boy looked at his dad and his lower lip pushed out as he started to cry.

"I can't push it Daddy," the boy said. "It hurts."

He scooped up the boy and bolted out the bedroom door and down the stairs. The boy put his right arms around his dad's neck but his left arm hung limp at his side.

"Are you guys ready for some breakfast?" his wife said as she heard the usual morning sound of her husband and son bounding down the stairs.

Her smile faded as she noticed the look on her husband's face. She had never seen that look before.

"Oh God what's wrong?"

"He's burning up and something is wrong with his left arm," he said as he headed for the back door of the house and the car. "I'm taking him to the doctor."

She could see panic in her husband's face as he jogged for the car, holding his son close to his chest as he ran. She knew something was terribly wrong. She had never seen that look of fear in his eyes. He wasn't one to be afraid.

"Wait! Wait! Oh God wait!" she hollered out as she ran after them. "What is wrong?" she said as she jumped into the car and took the little boy from him. He started the car and sped away kicking street gravel up in a spray as the tires grabbed at the graveled street.

The big black 1951 Ford® came to a screeching halt and double-parked in front of the doctor's office. He jumped out of the car opened the passenger side door and helped his wife and little boy out of the car. They hurried up the three steps that lead to the doctor's office waiting room. They didn't have to wait long. The country doctor saw them come through the door. The doctor knew real fear when he saw it.

"Bring him in," the old doctor said. He looked at the boy through his glasses, slid down on his nose, "aren't feeling so good, little guy?"

There was a trace of vomit on his dad's shoulder. The doctor touched the back of his hand to the boy's forehead as the father placed him on the examination table.

"I was playing with him this morning and noticed his left arm was hanging at his side and he couldn't hold onto anything with his left hand. I think he is running a fever and he just started to vomit a little."

"Here, young lad, grab hold of this stick," the doctor said as he held a tongue depressor for the young boy to grab. The boy couldn't do it. The doctor pulled the thermometer out of the boy's mouth and checked his temperature—105 degrees.

"I want you to take him to Saint Joseph Hospital in Sioux City right now," the country doctor said as he turned to the worried dad. "He could have polio. I'll call and make all the necessary arrangements. Keep wet towels on his forehead. I'll have the nurse get some for you."

"Polio?" the young dad said as he looked at his wife. "You think he has polio?"

"I am not going to take a chance," the doctor said. "The sooner you get him to Sioux City, the better chance he will have."

He looked at his wife, her lips quivered and her eyes were bulging out of her head. She looked at her little boy and back at her husband and then took him from his arms and pulled him next to her bosom.

"He can't have polio. He just has the flu. He can't have polio," she cried.

"Well, I hope you are right but let's not take the chance," the doctor said as he opened the door and called for his nurse.

"Get me some cold towels and some ice water," he told the nurse. "And get me a little coke syrup if we have any."

She was back in a minute or two and they started down the hall toward the front door. The nurse handed the dad the towels and a small bottle of coke syrup.

"If he starts to vomit a lot," the doctor said, "give him some of that syrup. The fewer people who come into contact with him now, the better the chances are that the infection won't spread."

"Get going but be careful," the doctor said as he walked them to the front door, "there is no time to waste."

Tears were running down her face and her bottom lip still quivered as she tried to understand what the doctor had told her. A war was on. Micro piranha where attacking inside of her son's body, eating away at him just like they would devour an innocent fawn who had stumbled into their waters.

The little boy put his right arm around her neck as they turned and started down the steps. The smell of medical alcohol filled the air as the nurses were busy trying to disinfect everything in the office.

The doctor made one last visual check of the little boy as he watched them hurry to the waiting car.

"There is a good chance we have detected it early enough that they can do something for him," the doctor hollered out.

She looked at the little boy's face during the hour-long drive to Sioux City. His hot beads of sweat were joined with her tears as she wept. She cradled the sick youngster in her arms brushing his blond hair. She wiped his brow with the cold towels. She was prepared to stay for as long as it would take.

His father switched his gaze from the road to his wife and boy. He watched their every move.

She held him tight and put her chin over the top of his head. If the Angel of Death was coming for her little boy, the angel would have to pry him loose from her arms.

"Are you the folks from Hartington?" the nurse asked.

"Yes," the father answered.

"Your son will be placed in a special unit so you will need to come with me back outside. We will be going to a special white building beside the hospital. They are waiting for us there. Please put these on," she said as she handed them white cotton masks. The nurse put on some gloves and put a mask on the boy. He shook from chills.

The plain white building had a heavy metal door and one picture window. Above the door was a sign, Isolation Ward-Authorized Medical Personnel Only. To the right of the door was a button with a sign that read, "push for service."

The nurse pushed the button and the door soon opened.

"Is this the Hartington boy?" the doctor at the door asked.

"Yes," the nurse answered.

The doctor reached out for the boy. The boy's mother pulled her son away.

"I'll carry him in," his mother said.

"I'm sorry," the doctor replied. "The infection risk is too high for you to come in. We'll take good care of him."

"No," she cried as she pulled him tight against her chest. "I'm coming in with him."

"I'm sorry," the doctor said sternly, "you can't come in."

"Give him to me," her husband said as he turned to his wife. "We are wasting time. Give him to me!"

She looked at him. She could see the stern look in his eyes. She looked at her son, now covered with sweat and shaking from fever. She released her grip ever so gently as her husband took him from her arms and handed him to the doctor.

"As soon as we know something, we'll let you know," the doctor said as he took the boy. "There is a waiting room in the main hospital. Someone will meet you there and explain everything. We have to go now."

The doctor gently held the boy against his chest, wrapped the blanket around his body and turned away, the door closing behind him.

They went back to the main hospital and waited for most of the day before word came.

"Your son does have polio," another doctor said as he looked up from the chart. "There isn't much we can do for him right now but make him comfortable and let the fever run its course. It appears his left side is involved."

"Will he be OK?" the anxious dad asked.

"We don't know right now. It's just too early to tell," the doctor said as he took off his glasses and sat on the edge of the magazine covered coffee table. "We'll just have to wait and see."

"He isn't going to die is he?"

"I don't think so. He seems like a strong little guy and has a great will to live. There will be some damage but it is too early to tell what and how much damage there will be."

Nothing would be known for a couple of days and there was no place for them to stay. The doctor told them to go home. Since polio was an epidemic, they would be quarantined for two weeks to be sure they had not caught it. They would be modern day lepers trapped in their own home, not able to be with their boy now gripped by a disease without a cure.

If he lived through the next critical days they could soon stand in front of a one way mirror, which faced a playroom, and watch him play with the hospital toys. At his age of three, it wasn't long before he forgot who his parents were even though they spent days looking through that one way glass. For all practical purposes, his doctor became his dad and his nurse became his mom.

The doctors watched and battled as the disease took aim at various muscle groups in the young boy's body. The damage was done. Unlike so many others, he would live. He would walk again. This little boy would never be perfect but he would be lucky. Finally, the hospital called. Their son could come home. They could begin their long journey back to normal.

"He'll need daily physical therapy so the muscles in his back and legs don't atrophy," the doctor said. "Our physical therapist will show you what to do and give you a schedule when you should do it."

"What are the long term effects going to be?"

"He won't have much mobility in his left arm and hand," the doctor continued. "When he is a little older we may be able to help him with some orthopedic surgery. We may be able to rebuild his hand and arm to give him more use of his hand and increase his gripping power, but for now, we must concentrate on trying to build up what muscles we can."

"Will this therapy be painful for him?"

"Yes, but it absolutely has to be done or he may not be able to walk. There is a great little guy in that little damaged body," the doctor continued. "He has been the darling of the ward. All you have to do is reach down deep inside and help him bring out his best. They will bring him over here in a few minutes. Best of luck to you."

"Thank you for everything doctor," the dad replied.

As the doctor walked down the hall, the double doors to the main hospital opened. He looked at the sun filled hallway and could see a nurse and a little boy walking toward them.

He slowly stood up and watched as the little guy and his nurse made his way toward them.

"Here he comes," he said as he reached down and touched his wife's shoulder. She turned suddenly and got up. She started down the hallway toward the boy.

"Wait," he said as he sank down to one knee, "wait, please wait."

The boy walked slowly, almost with a stumble as the nurse bent over and watched his every move so he wouldn't fall.

"Hey little man," he said as the boy got closer. "Ready to go home?"

The boy stopped, looked up at the nurse as though he was asking for permission to speak and look at the man kneeling in front of him. He hadn't seen this man or this woman for six months.

"Go ahead," the nurse said. "It's your daddy, go ahead."

He dropped his grip on the nurse's hand and stood by himself. He gathered his balance and looked at his dad. He looked at his boy. He could see fear and confusion in the little boy's eyes as he struggled to stand. He tried not to look at the metal braces on his legs and the brace on his left arm. His heart sank to his feet but he knew he couldn't let his son see it. He couldn't let this little guy know he wasn't anything other than little man. His little man. He stopped his tears and held out his arms.

"Come on little man," he said. "Let's go have some breakfast."

The boy smiled and shuffled toward his dad falling into his arms. He picked his son up spun him around until the boy started to giggle—the same way he giggled when his dad chased him around the house.

He would be part of his son's struggle. He would be his mental crutch until the day his son could throw his self doubts away. He would give him his strength until he could develop strength of his own. He knew his son would face mountains but he would teach him how to climb. He would hold this son up to the gentle wind and if his son wanted to fly, he would release him to freedom. His son was finally coming home. He was alive and safe and free to forever play in the grateful soul of his dad.

"Daddy," the boy said as they cleared the front door of the hospital, "can we have oatmeal for breakfast?"

"You want to have oatmeal, little man?"

"Uh huh," the boy said as he put his wrapped and braced left arm around his dad's neck. "I need oatmeal so I can be a big and strong quarterback."

The Invasion
of the City Boys

◆

Five miles West of Hartington, Nebraska was one of the most special places in the world for this mother of three very active young boys. Unlike most farms, this one was tucked away on a hillside off of a narrow graveled road. The farm belonged to Hjalmer (pronounced "Hi-yell-mer") and Irene Johnson. Irene was her sister.

Her three boys, ages six, eight, and ten, were full of energy and loved to go to the farm. Hjalmer was just a bit tough to say so the boys called him Uncle Jelly. While they were in a name-changing mood, Irene became Aunt Rebe.

"Are we there, Mom?" her oldest boy hollered out from the back seat.

"Look for the Rose Hill School so I know where to turn," she instructed her busy sons as she fought the steering wheel of the old Ford® as it bounced along the muddy ruts in the road.

"I see it," the oldest boy said.

"I seen it first!" her middle son yelled out.

"No you didn't," the older brother challenged. "I saw it first."

"Mom, make him stop pushing me," cried out her youngest son as the pushing match erupted in the back seat.

"This is where your dad and I went to school," she said as the car moved within viewing distance of the old one room school.

"We walked several miles to school when we were little kids," she said as she waved her hand toward the endless cornfields. "We walked in the mud and the snow to get our education."

It was late fall and the harvesting was almost complete. The hillsides were covered with the short brown stalks, evidence the corn picker collected the success of the season. The season was about to change. The cold night temperatures put a crust of thin ice over the mud and water and it wouldn't be long before this farm would be isolated from much of the world. Winter would return the land to the flow it once had, covering the roads with huge drifts of impassable white snow.

As she turned the car onto the graveled road, she still had some precision driving in front of her. She had to navigate the ruts to a rickety old metal bridge that crossed a sometimes non-existent creek. Right after the bridge was Uncle Jelly's lane.

The lane followed the flow of the hills. The lane went down through a little bog caused by drainage from the farm pond. She pushed in the clutch and shifted to second gear so she could get a good load of steam and plow on through the snow and mud and reach higher ground on the other side. Once across the bog, it was a quick trip up a short hill to a beckoning bunch of stately cottonwood trees. They stood bare ready to battle the cold north winds of winter.

"Now you kids leave stuff alone and be good," she said as the boys jumped out of the car. "Stay close by and don't get into anything." The boys jumped out of the car and hurried up the hill toward the barn.

"Can this kitten walk on ice?" the little brother asked as he picked up the small kitten that came out of the barn to see what all the noise was about.

"Sure," his older brother said as he turned his attention to a calf walking up to the fence by the barn.

The little boy put the kitten on the horse watering tank ice and watched and laughed as the kitten slipped and scrambled on the ice.

"Come here," the little boy said as he pulled himself up on he edge of the horse tank. He leaned over the edge and reached out for the kitten. As the little boy reached out, he lost his balance and put his hand on the ice. His brother jumped around as he heard the thin ice snap.

"Don't!" his brother screamed as he looked back and ran toward the tank just as the ice broke. He caught his little brother by the seat of his pants as the ice gave way to the cold water below. It was too late for the kitten as it slid under the slab of ice. The older brother pushed on the ice slab, frantically trying to reach the trapped kitten in the cold water under the ice.

"He can't get out!" the little brother screamed and cried. The kitten was gone.

"You boys get away from that horse tank," the boy's mother hollered out as she reacted to the noise coming from the top of the hill.

She could see the older boy reach into the tank and pull something from the cold water.

"Come here this minute!" she hollered as she threw down her red checkered apron and started out the porch door. "Did you put a kitten in the horse tank?" she questioned he youngest son. The crying boy could do nothing more than bob his head up and down.

"Oh mercy, mercy. Look what you have done! The poor thing. You've drowned Uncle Jelly's kitten. Now march out there and tell him you're sorry," she ordered as she pointed to his uncle driving his small Ford® tractor in from the field. "Do it right this minute!"

The little boy's lower lip was sticking out and quivering. He had to confess to the most terrible thing he had ever done.

The boy's uncle stood just a few inches over five feet tall and was a little round at the middle. The hot Nebraska summer sun baked great lines into his face and the twinkle in his eye shined through his wire frame glasses. This was the man who would administer punishment to this shaking little boy with the very pronounced lower lip. He kneeled down next to the boy and took the dead kitten out of the boy's hands.

"Let's see if we can find a small box," he said as he put his rough but gentle hand on his youngest nephew's head. "We'll put the little kitten in it and take him over there under the big trees and give him a proper burial. I think if you say a little prayer, God will take him to Heaven right away. Wouldn't you like that?"

The youngster nodded his head in agreement and together the uncle and the boy dug a small grave under a big cottonwood tree and buried the kitten with the same tenderness, prayers and tears that most folks save for family.

Later in the day, the gentle uncle didn't get angry when the oldest boy sawed off one of the legs of his best wooden ladder. His uncle just sat down with the boy, showed him how to measure, and then helped him saw off the other leg. Once again the ladder was perfect but his farmer friends might wonder why the first rung was right on the ground.

The boy's Aunt Rebe had the same gentle kindness. She stood in her kitchen wearing her apron. She handed out fresh baked oatmeal cookies along with a long soft "Ohhhhhhhhhhhh," when she was suppose to be amazed by one of boy's amazing farm country discoveries. She made time for them during the summer and took them out behind the house, right to the property line and lifted the little ones up to the lower branches of the mulberry trees.

"Don't eat the ones with the white stuff on them," she cautioned. An assortment of Nebraska birds also shared the grove and loved mulberries, too.

"If we can find a whip in here, we can play Zorro®," the middle boy told his younger brother. The boy searched the machine shed until he spotted a bunch of leather straps hanging from the rafters. He crawled up on a barrel and pulled at the leather straps until one of the pieces fell in front of him.

"This is perfect! Give me those hedge clippers."

His little brother handed him the clippers and he cut the strap free and let it fall to the floor. He jumped off the barrel and threw the clippers on the floor, picked up the strap and snapped it over his head. The snap hit his brother on the arm.

"Mom!" the little boy cried out as he ran down the hill bawling, holding the red welt on his arm. "Look Mom, he snapped me with a whip!"

Big trouble was brewing for Zorro®. "Did you snap your little brother with some kind of whip? Where did you get this whip?"

"Ah but Mom…Ah but Mom…" he protested

"Show me this minute! Hughaaaaaaaaaaaaaaaaaah." she gasped. "Did you cut that off of Uncle Jelly's antique harness?"

"Ahbut Mom," he could see his Uncle Jelly and Aunt Rebe standing in the machine shed doorway. He could tell that harness meant a great deal to his Uncle and Aunt. It was part of their farm pioneer past.

"I'm sorry Uncle Jelly," he said as he fought back the tears.

In the late 1960's, things changed. No one really knew the reason. Maybe farming was getting to be a little too tough. For whatever the reason, the news was soon plastered all over town.

"Farm Auction," the sale bill headline blared. Everything was there. Tractor. Short ladder. Good harness with some repairs necessary. Household furniture. Uncle Jelly and Aunt Rebe were giving up the farm. The boy's mom went out to the farm without her now prize teenage boys. She helped get everything organized. Sale day came and everything was neatly arranged from the top of the hill by the horse tank, all the way down to the house. The teenage Zorro® went to the sale with his dad.

"Just keep your hands and arms low and don't wave at anybody or nod your head when the auction starts," his dad instructed. A small crowd milled around until the designated hour when a short man with a very deep voice got on top of a hay wagon.

"Gimmie ten, willyaten, ten, hup! eleven…" the auctioneer hollered out in a rhythmic deep rumble as he pointed his cane to the line of assembled items. The teenager was amazed how fast his Uncle Jelly and

Aunt Rebe's possession disappeared into the waiting cars and pickups. The story of a lifetime was gone with the simple wave of a hand.

"Folks," the auctioneer said as he stopped right in the middle of trying to auction the tractor, "Jelly took better care of this tractor than he did his wife! Now what am I bid?" As usual, he got more money.

Finally, the auction was over and everything was gone. Stillness gripped this once exciting place. There wasn't a sound other than the rustling of the cottonwood leaves from the summer winds and the distant crow of a pheasant saying good-bye. Everyone was gone and nothing remained but the house, the barn, the out buildings, and under one large cottonwood tree, a small dirt mound covered with some fresh cut spring daisies.

Fireworks
from Number Three

———————————— ◆ ————————————

A group of community spirited men and women wanted to create a special social gathering place for sport and fun. They wanted to be sure anyone who wanted to be part of the new Town and Country Club could be. All a person had to do was pay dues and pitch in. These community leaders wanted nothing to do with a snobby golf club. What they wanted was a place where families could go and have fun celebrating holidays and family occasions. They wanted a special place where they could take out-of-town friends and blow their socks off. Heavy equipment pushed the 160 acres of pastureland around until the fairways were cut and the mounds of dirt for the greens were in place. The clubhouse started as a metal building shell.

"Wouldn't it be nice to have a full length screened porch so folks could sit out on a nice spring or summer day and enjoy a drink, watch people finish the ninth hole or just have a neighborly chat with whomever might wander in?"

Simple suggestions from nice people produced a pretty nice place. You could not walk into this clubhouse and not have folks know who you were. That would not be up to neighborly standards. Come in. Get comfortable. Enjoy your day.

There was no free ride, however. You had to pay dues to become a member. A family wanting to be part of the initial country club venture had to shell out $100 in early 1950 dollars to buy a share of stock—only one share of stock per family. Stock was not transferable. With that kind of arrangement, no one had more say than anyone else did and the snobbishness went on down the road to the bigger towns.

The members elected a president, vice president, and secretary-treasurer each year. And, of course, new people could be placed in office each year unless folks re-elected the people in place because of the good work they were doing. Bad work and you were out. Things clicked right along at a very friendly pace with those arrangements.

The golf course side of things was a little different. The city owned it. They paid for the people to take care of it. They bought the fertilizer and the equipment and they charged an annual membership fee. You could play all of the golf your little heart desired for under $100 a year. Everyone in the immediate family could play for that fee.

There were special activities for all. Tuesday morning was junior golf day—kids older than eleven only, please. Lessons were offered. Nine holes were played. Prizes were awarded. Lunch was served. Everybody off the course by noon so the retired men could play.

Wednesday was Ladies Day and Ladies Day meant Ladies Day. If you were a man and if it had been raining for two weeks solid and the only nice day was Wednesday, you did not play golf. No exceptions. Ladies Day at the golf course was a more holy day than Easter and maybe better attended than the Easter services.

"Dad," the young boy said as he walked into the kitchen and noticed all of the extra special goodies prepared on trays, "is mom serving at Ladies Day this week?"

"Don't touch that!" she hollered from the laundry room as she rushed in to protect her precious finger foods from young hungry fingers. Her recipes and reputation were on the line when it was her turn to serve at Ladies Day.

Two or three members prepared the Ladies Day Lunch and the duty was passed throughout the membership throughout the summer season. The last thing in the world a respectable local lady wanted to do was feed some slop to the rest of the girls. The search was always on for a new recipe and each family in town had to try it out until it was perfected before it went out to the club house for Ladies Day.

She was a little touchy when her week arrived. Her kitchen was a research facility for a week prior to Ladies Day. The house was full of smells and food forms the family would not see for at least another year.

"Keep your glomhooks out of those Tupperware® containers—they are for Ladies Day!" she ordered as she rushed around the kitchen, her fully loaded gas stove, and stuffed refrigerator.

"But I am hungry, Mom."

"Make a peanut butter sandwich."

"But why can't I have one of these little triangle sandwiches with the crust cut off?"

"They're for Ladies Day."

"Well how about a piece of one of those lemon meringue pies in the back fridge?"

"They are for Ladies Day."

"Mom, you really don't love me anymore, do you?" the boy asked as he stood over the trays of goodies.

"Sure I love you honey. Now make a peanut butter sandwich and stay away from the Ladies Day food."

Her boys didn't understand the art of proper food presentation. They only appreciated taste.

"Mom, why do you only put one little piece of lettuce on that salad plate?" he asked.

She hardly noticed him as she set about creating her salads. Best salad plate. Healthy looking lettuce leaf. Special layered Jell-O® creation from a special mold. Special topping.

"Wow Mom, that looks pretty neat."

She smiled as she gently created each salad and put the filled trays into any refrigerator space she could find. She was ready to go as soon as her husband walked through the door.

"Help me take this food up to the country club."

He looked at the trays of salads, the mounds of Tupperware® and the six lemon meringue pies and the helpful looking son with the filthy hands standing next to him.

"Go wash your hands," he said to his son.

He had a problem. None of this stuff dare change from the time it left the house until it was placed under the nose of one of the fifty or so ladies that would instantly judge her week of work. He had curved car seats. One quick stop and the salads could slide south, the meringue could fly off, and her dreams of praise and glory could be ruined. This was one of the most difficult challenges he faced each year. His helpful young son was back with clean hands and eager to help. He looked down at the boy looking up at him.

"You know, if we drop anything or mess anything up, we're both dead."

The boy bobbed his head up and down. He understood the risks. He still wanted to help.

"OK," he told his son, "you take the Tupperware® and I will get the pies."

"Please don't drop anything," she said.

"We won't."

"Please don't stop fast and ruin the meringue on the pies."

"I won't."

"Please make sure the salad plates sit on the center of the seat so they don't spill."

"I will."

"Would you like me to go along and hold some of the pies?"

"That would be nice."

"Maybe we should make two trips?"

"We can do that."

"I've worked so hard all week and I would hate to ruin these things just to take everything in one trip."

"We'll make two trips."

"I hope all of these things will turn out nice tomorrow."

"I am sure they will."

"I have been so busy I haven't had time to get to the beauty shop. I wonder if they can take me tonight?"

"Your hair looks fine. You'll be fine."

"I hope so," she said as she primped and looked into the mirror. Most of the local ladies got all dressed up for Ladies Day, unless the participating lady planned to play golf. Out-of-town guests were always taken to Ladies Day, female ones at least, and a guest could be assured of a warm welcome and a proper fuss. After lunch was cleared, it was bridge and golf time. Widows had their place on Wednesday and they would not miss bridge for the world.

Around four o'clock in the afternoon on Thursday, the parking lot at the club began to fill with men. By five it was full of cars and the local businessmen, farmers, and tradesmen were heading for the first and third tees for the weekly men's stag. There were three men per team and each team was composed of an "A", or good golfer; a "B" or not bad golfer; and a "C" or a "he needs work" golfer. There were nineteen teams in the league or fifty-four golfers on the course and one team in the kitchen fixing a mound of hamburger, chopping onions, and baking beans for the feed after golf.

Unlike the ladies, none of the men gave a damn about cuisine—a good thick hamburger and plenty of pork and beans dripping off a flimsy paper plate in one hand and a beer in the other was good enough. After golf came stories and beer, and some say, a little high stakes poker game. If you were a bridge player, you might find a game, too.

Holidays and Sundays were reserved for family outings and Sunday afternoon was the one time of the week where most golfing husbands and golfing wives found time to play golf with each other. Spontaneous events happened on Sunday afternoon.

"Let's have a couples handicap tournament."

"Oh, that sounds like fun. Everyone come about three and we'll play."

Lenyce came too. She was an elderly lady hoping to find a partner to play with her. She was the local society reporter for the Cedar County News. Her column often told who went where and who poured. A good time was had by all.

She had a wood, a couple of irons and a putter. She was short, kind of round, and still believed a lady wore a dress all of the time, even to play golf. She brought her club back, laid in across her shoulder, and with a mighty round house whack, the ball bounced down the fairway, straight and true, about fifty yards.

"Get your clubs and come play with Lenyce," she told her teenage son. "She loves to play but she needs a partner to play in the tournament."

"Awe Mom."

"Go on. Get your clubs. It won't hurt you a bit."

"Awe Mom, she only hits the ball about ten feet."

"But she hits it ten feet down the middle."

"Get your clubs. Hurry."

"We've found you a partner, Lenyce," she said as she came up to the elderly lady sitting alone in one of the porch chairs, wearing a straw bonnet and sun glasses.

"Oh? Who?"

"He's right there and ready to go. You two can play with Bud and Florence."

She looked around and saw the strapping teenager tying his black and white golf shoes. She put on her tattered brown ones and headed for the tee.

"I get to play with you?"

"Yup," the boy said as he cracked a smile. "And we are going to win."

The sports section of the Cedar County News carried the results. "Local teen and society editor take handicap tourney by ten strokes."

Sunday breakfast was another excellent choice if a family had out-of-town guests. Once again, out-of-town guests could also be assured of a warm greeting and a proper fuss. Most of the local widows wouldn't miss the breakfast either. The committee style system made it work. Two husband and wife teams were in charge of preparing the breakfast. The presentation was between the doilies of Ladies Day and the bean dripping plates of the men's stag. Eggs, your choice. Bacon or sausage and plenty of it. Pancakes, sometimes with a little cigar ashes mixed in when a certain cook was part of the volunteer team, legendary rolls and donuts from the wonderful local bakery and of course plenty of coffee, milk and juice. Breakfast started at eight and ended by noon. The idea was to take your family to church and after church, come out to the club and have breakfast. One of the committee members sat at a small card table and collected the minimal cost per plate—usually one to two dollars a serving. You were welcome to choose a nice card table for four or you could sit with another family at one of the large folding tables which seated eight, unless of course, there were more than eight members in the family.

Sunday morning is when those manners discussions at home turned in to practical application.

"Don't forget, you speak to adults as Mr. and Mrs. or Miss. No belching. Don't talk with your mouth full. Don't try to eat an entire pancake with one bite."

"We know Mom. We're not a bunch of animals."

"Could have fooled me," the father said as he parked the car. "Out."

Young boys with white shirts, black pants, black ties, and bulging eyes learned it was possible to carry a full plate of food and a glass of juice without spilling a single bit. They learned they could eat without belching. They learned they could chew with their mouths closed and people would notice their impeccable manners and polite behavior. This is where young reputations started to form.

"They have such nice boys," one of the elderly ladies remarked.

The best day was the Fourth of July. In the early days, the Fourth was a pot luck event. All of the member families came to the club complete with each wife's special covered dish. Regardless of the size of the crowd, there always seemed to be just the right amount of meats, vegetable, and desserts. The Fourth was an all day event for everyone however most folks started to gather around four in the afternoon.

Fathers and sons moved porch chairs outside so the large screened porch could be used for the covered dish buffet serving line. The ladies took care of all of the serving details while most of the men played golf.

For the youngsters, the rules were simple. Don't pick your nose. Stay out of the mud. Don't get grass stains on your pants. Be sure to call every adult by the appropriate Mr. or Mrs. and don't light any firecrackers around people. And, of course, don't go anywhere without first asking your mother or father.

Within ten minutes of the five-minute lecture, a herd of young boys were on the way down the steep bank behind the clubhouse and slogging their way through the nettles, mud and cow droppings to Little Creek.

At its widest, Little Creek was not more than a short run and a good jump to get across. If your jump was a little short, you might land in the dark gooey mud which was right next to the water and often covered with dragon flies, regular flies, and the worst of all, the big biting horse fly.

The boys didn't set off on this venture just to creek hop. They were on the way to Cedar County's answer to Mt. Everest. The local Mt. Everest was really half a hill that the creek had slowly eroded. The result was Clay Mountain, a high creek bank mountain just perfect for young boys to practice their climbing skill.

Little Creek made a gentle turn below Clay Mountain and this was where it tried to become deep and wide. Little Creek was no longer a two foot wide trickle you could cross with a run and a jump. It was four feet wide and maybe a foot or two deep.

"You're too little to climb Clay Mountain," he told his younger brother who was tagging along as best he could.

"I am not. I can climb it just as good as you."

"No you can't. You'll fall right down into the gooey stink mud and the horse flies will eat you to death."

"I won't fall into any goo mud."

"You will too. Now just stay there."

The older boys started their climb up the clay embankment, grabbing clumps of dirt that had not given way to the rains of summer. Each chose a different path to try to be the first one to the top—the King of Clay Mountain.

"Ahhaaa!" one of the boys hollered as his handhold gave way. He tumbled backwards and down the clay, into the dirt below, and rolled through the mud into the dirty stream.

"Mom is going to kill you," the younger brother said as he looked at him. "You are going to smell like cow pee."

The mountain climbing boys all knew the potluck supper would begin around six in the evening so things could be cleared off and everyone could be in "ooh" and "ahhh" position by the time darkness set in. There was a certain order which people approached the serving line. The older ladies went through the line first followed by the mothers with small children and then by dads and others.

The enormous selection was personally stressful for a number of the pot luck cooks. The worst thing that could happen was to have your covered dish still covered while your neighbor down the street had a dish that was almost licked clean.

"Eat your mom's chicken," he whispered to his boys.

"Where is it, Dad?"

"The pan at the end."

"There isn't any chicken left in that pan, Dad."

"Good. Eat anything you want, then."

"Why hello there," said the very tall and always gracious Mrs. Robinson. "How are you boys tonight?"

"Just fine Mrs. Robinson," the oldest boy answered as he tried to hold that thin paper plate before the chicken leg and the Jell-O® rolled off one of the weak sides.

"Tell your mother her chicken was just wonderful."

"I will."

"She is such a good cook, you know."

"Yes. We know. Have you ever had any of that stuff she makes for Ladies Day?"

"Yes. It's always very good."

"All we get his peanut butter sandwiches. She gets really mad at us if we stick our fingers in the pies."

"That's a mighty full plate your have there, young man." He looked back, still trying to balance the chicken and the Jell-O® and acknowledged his dad's best friend.

"Hi."

"I never ate a big plate of food like that," he told the youngster as he chuckled. The boy looked at the big belly hanging over his belt and pushing against the buttons of his white shirt

"Nooooowwww Bud, yyyyyooooouuuu know that's a lie," his slow talking wife said as she corrected him in her famous blunt fashion.

Bud moved around at a fairly good pace. He was one of the prime movers and shakers in the country club and was always willing to ad his vision to the various betterment projects. He was always in a jovial mood except when he played golf. If he had a bad round, it was best to stay out of the way and out of earshot.

"God damn woman's game!" he was known to holler as he came into the clubhouse bar. He didn't always make it back to the clubhouse with a full set of clubs. He let one fly on the eighth hole and it landed in the top of a cottonwood tree.

"That's the last time I play this damn sissy's game."

The next day, a power company truck with cherry picker lift came out to the golf course and one of the his men fished the club out of the top of the tall cottonwood.

His wife Florence loved the game and played often. Her game temperament was just the opposite of her husband and so was the speed she played. She was also left-handed and an early golfing civil right worker. She was a major influence in organizing and promoting a left-handed tournament complete with a left-handed dinner where silverware was reversed, or in her and other lefties minds, where it should be in the first place.

Finally, food eaten, mess cleared away, and old ladies seated out in front of the clubhouse in the metal chairs, darkness had reached that magic time. It was time for the volunteer firemen to do their safe and spectacular stuff.

"Whoomp" went the sound as a little stream of light sparkled skyward from the top of number three fairway.

"Kaboom" went the first blast of earth shattering sound.

"Oh!" went the old ladies as they were suddenly stunned by the sound.

"Whoomp" went the sound again as another small stream of light header skyward followed by a "kapop pop pop" and streams of blue and red light lit up the night sky.

"Ooooh" sighed the excited crowd.

The show went on for fifteen minutes or so and finally the night sky went black and quiet again. The cars parked around the road in the park showed their appreciation by honking their horns and the assembled country club crowd cheered and whistled. The Forth of July passed again and little boys became a little better at being nice young gentlemen.

"Come on boys," she called to her three pride and joys. "Let's go home."

"Good night Mr. and Mrs. Robinson. Good night Mr. and Mrs. Rahn. Good night Mr. and Mrs. Zimmer." The youngsters put on their social best as the family moved from the clubhouse to the dark parking lot and the family car.

"I'm so proud of how you boys acted today," she said with a smile and an arm full of empty covered dishes. "People said some nice things about how polite you were."

"By the way, do any of you three polite gentlemen know how that bull snake got into the ladies locker room?" the dad asked.

"Must have crawled up from Clay Mountain or got scared of the fireworks, Dad,"

"I suppose," he said as he watched his youngest boy scratch his horse fly bite, and pull at his wet clammy shirt. "I suppose."

Old Henry

◆

They were standing next to the flower garden in the center of the park when the old man put his hand on the boy's shoulder.

"What did you say?" the old man asked.

"Where do flowers get their color?

The old man stopped weeding his prize tulips and pushed his Fedora® style straw hat back on his forehead.

"You mean the color of these tulips?" the old man asked as he mopped his brow with a big red bandanna handkerchief. Old Henry had a ruddy red weathered face whose deep lines formed and baked over many hot summers.

"Where does the yellow and red and pink come from?" the boy asked again. " The ground? That white stuff you put on them? Where does the color come from?"

"Take this end of the hose and go hook it up to that faucet," Henry told the boy as he pointed at a pipe sticking out of the ground about ten feet away. "We'll see if we can find the color."

Old Henry had a big job as the park caretaker. He fixed and painted benches. He picked up trash. He mowed acres of grass and hand trimmed two miles of hedge that marked the park's roadway. He never seemed to have an organized plan but everything got done and he always found time for the boy.

Henry took a brass nozzle from the back pocket of his farmer style bib overalls and attached it to the hose. "All set?" he asked the boy. The boy bobbed his head yes. "Turn it on and come here."

The boy turned the handle and the hose jumped like a striking snake from the faucet to Old Henry's hand. Water started to drip from the nozzle.

"Here, hold the hose in your left hand and turn the nozzle with your right hand until it forms a mist," he told the boy.

"Like this?" the boy asked as the stream from the nozzle turned into a mist spray as he turned it.

"That's just right," Henry told the smiling boy looking up at him. "Now aim the spray high above the flowers." The boy aimed the spray high into the dark blue afternoon Nebraska sky.

"Look through the mist and tell me what you see."

The boy did as his friend asked. He squinted and looked carefully at the sky, not exactly sure what he was suppose to see.

"There's a rainbow, Henry!"

"That's where the flowers reach up and get their color," the old man said as he chuckled.

Old Henry's laugh an unhurried slow deep chuckle. The boy was sure the old man's chuckle had to be directly connected to that round belly which danced when the old man laughed. He laughed at the old man's slow belly bouncing chuckle. He liked his gentleness. The boy stood and watched the rainbow through the mist. He had no doubt that his old friend was telling him the truth.

With the watering work done, Old Henry and the boy walked over to his old tan and brown DeSoto® and carefully cleaned and sharpened all of his tools.

"Do you always put oil on those tools?" the boy asked.

"Always," the old man said as he scraped the dirt from the spade, sharpened the end, and coated it with oil. "If you take good care of your tools, they'll last a lifetime."

"Do you always put them in the same place in your trunk?"

"Always," he said as he smiled. "That's called being organized. You don't need much room when you're organized. It's not as hot today as I thought it would be today," he said as he opened the passenger door of the old DeSoto®, reached into a bucket of ice water, and pulled out two bottles of grape NeHi®. "I had planned to drink both of these but I think one will be enough. Why don't you have this one? Let's sit under that big elm tree and drink these."

Summer passed and the boy learned all sorts of interesting things. You could see some of the boy's work in spots of unevenly trimmed hedge. The new paint on the six foot green fence at the ballpark didn't quite reach the top of the fence. Two spots of grass were starting to wear thin under the big elm tree and Henry always seemed to have an extra grape NeHi® in the ice water bucket.

"Mom, Thanksgiving is for families isn't it?" the boy asked as she kneaded the bread for the holiday rolls.

"Why sure, honey," she said, "and it's for being thankful for lots of things."

"That's good," he said as he looked up at her and smiled. "I am thankful for Old Henry. He doesn't have a family you know. Can we make him part of our Thanksgiving?"

"Sure, honey," she said. "We have plenty of food. You ask him."

Around noon on Thanksgiving, the brown DeSoto® pulled up in front of the big gray two-story house. Inside, a table for six waited with a complete Thanksgiving dinner of turkey, dressing, sweet corn, fresh baked bread, cranberry salad, and pumpkin pie with whipped cream.

"Sit next to me, Henry," the boy said as he walked into the formal dining room with his friend.

"Thanks for having me, Bun," he said to the boy's mother. "Everything looks just fine. It's been a long time since I have eaten such a good meal."

Christmas brought the same spirit from the boy. His mom was a great cookie baker.

"Let's not stay long," she whispered as she looked at the dusty hall floor and the unpainted walls of the upstairs apartment hallway located above the feed store. The hall was dark and smelled like the inside of a Cherrio's® box. The boy knocked on the door and soon Old Henry was standing there smoking his gooseneck pipe. The smell of pipe tobacco filled the apartment air.

"Hi Henry! Merry Christmas!" the boy said as he handed the old man the carefully wrapped tray of Christmas cookies.

"Well Merry Christmas to you! Come in. Come in." His apartment was lighted by a single bulb at the end of a long cord hanging from the darkness of the ceiling. There were two brown wooden folding chairs with slatted backs, a hot plate, a small end table and a single bed in the corner.

"Mom," the boy said as they were going down the stairs, "how come Old Henry has to live in such a lonely place?"

"I don't know honey, but he seems happy and he looks healthy and those are the most important things. Plus," she said as she brushed her son's blond hair, "he has a good friend who remembers him."

In the years that followed, there were a few more shared Thanksgiving dinners and Christmas cookie trays. Old Henry retired and a new man started to take care of the park.

"Honey," his mom called out over the noise of all the folks gathered in the house for his high school graduation party, "look who's here."

He looked at the front door his mom held open. He could see a cane and a stooped over old man with a smile on his face and a twinkle in his eye coming through the door.

"Henry," he called out as he bolted toward the door and helped his old friend to a chair in the dining room.

"This is for you," the old man said as he reached into the top of his bib overalls and pulled out a white envelope. The boy opened the card.

"Congratulations," it read, "you'll do very well. Your friend, Henry."

"Thank you," he said as he gave his old friend a hug.

"What are your plans?" Henry asked.

"I'm going to college to study commercial art."

"I'm not surprised," he said. "You'll be very good at that."

It wasn't long before the boy graduated from college and became an East coast advertising agency artist.

"Your Mother is line two," his secretary told him as he punched the flashing telephone button. "Hi Mom," he said, "this is a treat."

"Honey," his Mother said on the other end of a long distance call, "Old Henry passed away today."

"God bless him," the young artist softly said as he hung up the phone and wiped his wet eyes with the palms of his hands.

"Thank you for showing me where the colors are."

Christmas

◆

"Go down and get the deer head" she ordered her second son seated at the kitchen table.

"Awe Mom, you aren't going to put up that stupid deer head again?" the boy pleaded.

"Get the Santa suit, too!" she sternly ordered.

He hated to go down in that basement. There we're all kinds of threats down there. There were shelves of old canned goods the family would probably never eat. Occasionally, he spotted a mouse or lager. And of course, give a cricket a quarter of an inch around an old warped wooden basement window and a tribe of the damn things would soon be jumping around and making their knee scratching noises.

The head was a magnificent buck with a five-point rack and was no doubt the bragging prize of some hunter of years gone by. The taxidermist mounted the prize deer's head with a slight proud uplifted turn to the right. No doubt he envisioned his handsome work would be prominently displayed over the fireplace hearth of some well-to-do hunter. Little did he know it would be the prize decoration of a Christmas loving housewife.

"Did you get the Santa suit?" she asked her young son as he struggled through the basement door with the musty old deer head.

"Awe Mom, you aren't going to do the Santa bit are you?" he pleaded again.

She didn't steal the mount from someone's mantle, she discovered him on top of the beer cooler in the Chief Bar, a local business her husband once owned. She also discovered an intriguing piece of electronics compliments of a liquor company. The flashing light display was designed to catch the attention of the bar patrons and suggest they buy a bottle of cordials, a line of after dinner sipping liqueurs made from everything from apricots to raspberries.

She saw instant possibilities in the flashing lights, particularly the large blinking red one in the center of the cardboard display. Take one moth-eaten deer head and tape a red blinking display light on the old deer's nose and you have nothing less than "Rudolph the red nosed reindeer...." hanging on the front porch of the small town Christmas wonderland house.

"Listen," she said as she and her son stood on the front porch ready to put up the Christmas display. "Can you hear the wind?"

"What wind, Mom?"

"Listen to the Rossiter pines," she said as she pointed across the street at the tall pines, which dominated the huge front lawn of the Rossiter house. "The trees will tell you when the snow is coming."

"Is it going to snow?" the boy asked as he looked at the big pines and listened to the wind gusts as they whistled through the big trees.

"It will snow soon," she said. "Let's get the old boy up and blinking. When we're finished with this, we can start on the cookies."

The boy smiled at his mom now standing on a folding chair with the deer head over her shoulder. She soon found the big nail and slid the mount on it. Next, she taped the red bulb to his nose. "OK, honey," she said to her son, "plug him in."

He plugged the cord into the outside electrical socket and the red nose started to flash. "There," she said. "It's Christmas."

She became a famous cookie maker in this small town. She made them to share them so her cookie trays were welcome holiday gifts. There were always her seasonal favorites including divinity, a wonderful white type of fudge; fudge with walnuts; and mice, a little licorice flavored crunchy cookie about the size of diet breadstick cut into half-inch chunks. She also made date bars covered with powdered sugar and a special bar made of chocolate chips, coconut, and dates baked into a light brown crust of brown sugar. The favorite of her helpful deer head-hanging son was her sugar cookies. She had every cookie cutter ever known to K-Mart®, Sears®, or any other store. When she finished making the great mound of sugar cookie dough, she took her prize rolling pin, carefully dusted it with flour, and rolled the now floured dough out on her large flour covered, only-for-cookie-cutting, heavy cloth. Once perfectly rolled and perfectly floured, she stepped cautiously back a step of two and let her perfect little darlings sons take over the cookie cutting and decorating process. The three boys attacked the waiting dough like feeding sharks.

Another favorite, which required the help of her three little angels, was a sugar cookie, about an inch and half in diameter, with a special chocolate mint center. Only special hard mints would do and if it meant driving the 120-mile round trip to Sioux City to find them, so be it. It would not be Christmas in this house without these special sugar cookies with the hard-to-find, chocolate mints baked inside. The boys would gladly give up the deer head and the stuffed Santa but it would never be Christmas unless they had a good fix of their mom's famous mint cookies.

The dog jumped and barked as the young boys teased her with rolled up pieces of cookie dough. Great cookie dough from the dog's point of view but it was a little hard on the Scottie's system. She especially liked a little hunk of warm fudge when one of the boys stuck it on top of her very active little black nose. Her red tongue went crazy and her head bounced wildly trying to reach the sweet prize.

"Look what he did to my Christmas tree, Mom!" protested the older son as the little guy decided his older brother's Christmas tree looked good enough to eat without baking and promptly did so.

"He got more that I did!" hollered her second son as he tried to push his bigger brother out of the way.

"Mom, make him give me the Santa cutter!" The little brother wanted to eat his brother's cookie and have his the cutter, too.

"Someone go find Uncle Bill and tell him to come up here," she ordered.

Her bachelor farmer brother had to be ordered or invited to the house. He was the family historian and guardian of ancient family tradition. Their roots went to the small town of Bergen, Norway and her bachelor brother knew the traditions and the roads that lead back to Norway.

She worried about her bachelor brother living on the old farm place. Nothing had changed at that old farm since she lived there as a girl. He wasn't a good housekeeper and she worried about what the neighbors would think. He didn't give a damn about what people thought of him as long as they were friendly enough to take time to visit.

"What is that smelly stuff?" the middle son asked as he entered the kitchen, climbed up on the footstool and looked at the boiling pot on the stove.

"Ludefisk," came the quick answer from his Uncle Bill as he sat at the kitchen table patiently waiting to be served his part of the traditional dinner. "It's what your ancestors had for Christmas dinner."

"This ain't no fish Uncle Bill, it's square and hard as a rock, and it ain't got no fins or head," he said with ten-year-old authority.

"Why sure it is. It's just been cleaned, cut up, and dried in the sun out by the sea," his uncle carefully explained as he pushed his Dekalb® seed corn hat toward the back of his head. He reached into the top part of his overalls for his can of Prince Velvet® leaf tobacco and a cigarette paper.

"Your ancestors were mostly fishermen and they had to dry the fish because they didn't have ice boxes like we have today," he explained as he held out the cigarette paper in front of his chin and carefully poured some strands of tobacco on the paper. The boy sat at the table with his uncle, grabbed a cookie, and started to munch as the family history lesson unfolded.

"When they got ready to eat the fish," the uncle continued as he licked one edge of the paper and formed a cigarette, "they soaked the dried fish and then boiled it in great big pots to make it tender, just like your mother is doing." The boy listened and watched as his uncle pulled a wooden match from one of the many pockets found on the top of a good set of dress overalls, struck the match on a brass button, and lit the loosely packed cigarette.

"In order to have fish for Christmas dinner, the fish would have to be dried to preserve it so they could save it from the fall to the winter," the wise uncle continued. "It had to stay out in the sun for days to get that hard, and the dogs might come by, have a little sniff, and pee on it."

"Mom!" the boy protested, "I ain't gonna eat any smelly fish that has dog pee on it!"

By then, the beloved Uncle was laughing so hard that small strands of lighted tobacco were being pushed out the business end of the home-made cigarette like a Roman candle, landing and burning his only good pair of overalls.

"What's in the sack, Dad?" one of the boys asked as his father came into the kitchen balancing a couple of brown grocery bags.

"Your dad is going to make his Christmas concoction," the boy's mother said as she knew it was time to give up her kitchen to her husband.

He sat the two bags on the counter, took off his coat, and started to unload his groceries. The first items to come out of the brown bag were eggs—dozens of eggs. The next items to come out were bags of powdered sugar. Then came pure creamery butter and finally a few bottles of vanilla extract.

"What are you going to do with all of those eggs, Dad?" the boy asked as he peered around his father.

"Crack them," he said.

"Why? You making cookies of something?"

"No," the father said as he opened the cardboard egg container. "I am making a drink."

"What kind of a drink, Dad?"

"An adult drink."

"The one that makes Uncle Jelly's nose all red?"

"Yup," the father said as he chuckled. "That's the one."

He wasn't very concerned about the clean kitchen floor or the spotless counter tops as he started to crack the eggs and pour the egg back and forth between the two shells until most of the white was in one half and the yoke was in the other half. Some of the whites didn't make the pass and ended up on his shirt, the counter, or the floor. The trusty dog helped clean the floor.

"Where's the nutmeg?" he asked his wife as he continued to trash her kitchen and ransack her cupboards.

He dumped the whites into the sink and put the perfect, unbroken yokes into a mixing bowl. After a dozen or so crack and sorts, he added his next ingredient, a few cups of powdered sugar. A measuring cup wasn't necessary. A coffee mug would do just fine. Last in was the butter and vanilla extract. Then, using his wife's magic wooden spoon, he blended all of the stuff into a smooth, yoke yellow batter. Next, he filled the whistling tea pot with water and put it on the stove. Out of another tall skinny brown paper sack came a quart of Old Crow®.

There was a special set of matching white mugs that she stored on the top shelf of one of her cupboards. She knew what was going on so the cups were washed and ready. As the teapot whistled away, he carefully measured a tablespoon of the secret stuff into each of the white mugs. Next was a shot of Old Crow®. He then filled the cup with boiling water and stirred the magic mixture until it was nice and smooth. When it passed his smell test, he dashed it with a little nutmeg. Presto! His famous Tom and Jerry known from downtown Hartington clear out to Bow Valley. A much different smell now filled the house. And, before long, so did a bunch of much happier looking neighbors, family, and friends. To bad the old deer couldn't have gotten a snoot-full of his Tom and Jerry adult delight. His musty smelling fur coat would have a much different smell and the snarling grin might have turned into a Christmas smile.

The boy's father made a roaring fire in the fireplace so the scene would be postcard perfect. He added a little color to the fire with a wax disk he bought in Sioux City. When he tossed one of those disks into the fire, the flames changed color. The jumping flames of green red and gold fascinated his young sons.

At the other end of the room, was the family Christmas tree. The tree had to be at least a six footer because that part of the living room had a little alcove of windows, which faced the street.

It took some doing for the boy's dad but he managed to arrange for Santa Claus to make an appearance on Christmas Eve. Santa never missed an appearance in those believer years but he put off most of the neighbors until later that night or sometime in the wee hours of the morning. This Santa was a little different from the one the boys visited at the big Sioux City department store a little earlier in the season. He wasn't as fat and his beard seemed to look more like cotton than a real beard. His voice seemed familiar even though the boys couldn't quite place it. And, this Santa didn't wear wire rim glasses. This Santa did have a better memory and knew the boy's names without being told. The other department store Santa had to ask. This Santa knew exactly what the boys wanted and delivered right on the spot! He was in and out with a flash.

In the blink of the old deer's electric red nose, the Christmas season was over. The long Nebraska winter lay ahead with the mountains of snow still to come, announced by the talking wind from the Rossiter trees. New sled tracks cut through the fresh snow on the golf course hills. New ice skates cut some clumsy curves across the rough ice on Little Creek. Bunnies ran from the bad shots from would-be young hunters and their new BB guns. And the short-legged Scottie made valiant attempts to make it out of the snowdrifts she was tossed into by her young keepers. The deer head went back to the basement shelf. And one boy would never eat fish that didn't come with fins.

The Dream Boat

$\blacklozenge$

"Mom," he said as he sat in the kitchen leaning his head on the kitchen table, "there's nothing to do."

"Well I have too much to do today to entertain you," she said. "Why don't you go to the library and get a book to read?"

"I don't want to read a book, Mom. I want something fun to do."

"Go fishing then."

"There aren't any fish in Little Creek and Bow Creek is too far. Plus, the crazy Judge may have some dynamite in the beaver dam again. He blows them up you know. Why don't you take Bill and me to Gavins Point."

"I," she said as she turned to put a tray of bread pans into the oven.

"Huh?"

"It's Bill and I, not Bill and me," she said, "and I still don't have enough time to take the two of you to Gavins Point. Find him and find something to do. Create your own adventures."

He got up from the kitchen table, slouched and put his hands in his pockets and shuffled slowly toward the back room.

"Pick up your feet," she ordered, "and no television. You can find something better to do that watch soap operas."

"There's nothing to do, Mom."

"Go find something to do, then."

He knew she wasn't going to see things his way so he headed for the back door. The black Scottie looked up from her cool place under the mud room table to see if her company was needed. He said nothing to the dog so she put her head back on her front paws and continued with her morning nap.

He pushed the door open and then the screen door and jumped past the step into the back yard.

"Shut the door," he head his Mom holler out. "The air conditioner is on. We're you born in a barn?"

He went back to the door and pulled it shut. The air conditioning was needed on a summer day like this one. It was already steamy at mid morning and the temperature would climb to record levels today. The pool wasn't open and he didn't feel like swimming anyway, at least not right now.

He picked his bike up from where he dropped it in the yard the night before, swung his leg over the boy's bar, and balanced the bike against his inner thighs. He put his hands on the handlebars and straightened his arms like a motorcycle daredevil. That Evil guy knew something about adventure but the closest thing any of his friends had to a motorcycle was Bob Fornash's motor scooter. He could almost outrun the motor scooter on foot.

He put his right foot on the pedal and pushed with his leg and was underway on his big trip to somewhere. The big elm trees shadowed the walk but soon he would be in the street and in squinting sunlight. He could turn left and head for the park. He could go right and maybe go out and see if he could tease a nearby farmer's donkey and make it chase him. He could go back and head for the golf course and hunt golf balls—they paid twenty-five cents for good ones, or he could head for downtown and just see what there was to see.

Downtown won. He pedaled harder, looked for traffic on Highway 15 and bolted across the street to the street that took him toward town. As he increased his speed, the noise from the playing card, attached to the bike frame with a clothespin, slapped against the spokes of his bike tire. If there was another bored kid within two blocks, he would hear him.

"Where are you going?" his friend Bill hollered out from his front yard. Bill was mowing the yard.

He rode his bike over to where his friend stood. The mower putted away, filling the air with a light cloud of white smoke. Bill reached down and pushed the metal tab against the spark plug, bringing the motor to a sputtering stop.

Bill finished his yard mowing chores. During this part of summer, there wasn't much yard left to mow. The heat turned the yard from green to brown and some folks were starting to talk about lost crops from drought. There hadn't been any significant moisture for weeks and the corn was starting to show signs of stress. The countryside needed a good drenching from a slow moving line of summer thunderstorms.

"Where are you going?" Bill asked.

"Downtown."

"What are young going to do downtown?"

"I don't know, maybe stop at Faulks Service Station and get a grape NeHi®."

"Wait, I'll go with you," Bill said as he pushed the mower toward the garage. He left the mower in the driveway next to where his bike lay. He dashed toward the front door of the house, pulled it open. "Mom, I am going to Faulks."

He slammed the front door without waiting for an answer, ran back to his bike and was soon riding down the street with his friend toward the filling station.

"What are you going to do today?" he asked his friend Bill.

"Don't know," he said and he pumped along, hands free, next to his friend. The playing cards chatted with each other as the two bikers rode down the street. They could feel the heat from the concrete as it radiated against the relentless sun.

They were soon at the station. They parked their bikes by the side of the building. Mr. Faulk wasn't in the outside pit changing oil, and no cars were parked at the two gas pumps. The boys opened the green wooden door to the small gas shack and went in. Mr. Faulk sat behind the glass case filled with candy bars, watching the day go by and keeping a close watch on his inventory of nickel treats. The red Coca-Cola® pop case was next to the door.

"Hello boys," Faulk said.

"Hi George." This was one adult the kids called by his first name and he didn't mind one bit. After all, there were plenty of places where kids could buy candy. Faulk's Service did exceptionally well. He didn't sell much gas and he didn't change much oil so candy was an important part of his business. Kids could call him whatever they liked as long as they had nickels and dimes to lay on the counter.

Bill lifted the top of the Coke® case. The bottles were submerged in cold water with only the caps visible. A metal plate with rows cut in it to fit just under the top of the bottle kept the pop inventory in a straight line, each line being a different type of pop. Strawberry. Orange. 7-Up®, Coke®, Grape NeHi®. Bill grabbed the top of a grape NeHi® bottle and slid it toward the right where all of the lines met another channel, which lead to a central mechanism. Put money in the slot and the mechanism would release letting the patron pull the bottle up and out of the cooler. Both boys spent their dime on grape NeHi®, used the opener attached to the side of the pop cooler to open the bottles and headed for the door.

"Just a minute you boys," George said as Bill opened the door. They stopped and looked at George and waited to hear what he had to say.

"If you are taking those bottle with you," he said, "you need to pay me a nickel bottle deposit."

"We're going to sit out here on the step and drink them."

"That's OK, but don't be running off thinking I won't notice."

"We won't George," Bill said. "We're scouts."

They sat down on the concrete step outside of the front door and started to drink the grape NeHi®.

"Ahh," Bill said as he took his first gulp. "That tastes good. Let's do something."

"What?"

"Go swimming."

"I can't swim."

"You can learn how."

"I don't want to swim today."

"Then lets go out to the creek and wade around and look for stuff."

"Too many leeches."

"Oh yea."

They sat for a few minutes drinking their pop and looking at the giant brick buildings across the street from the service station. In only four weeks, they would be making daily treks to school buildings. But for now, both buildings stood silent, their great lawns cut, and the breeze changing the light that filtered through the leaves and hit the glass on the buildings, reflecting the colors of summer.

"We need a big adventure."

"What kind of adventure?" Bill asked.

"Did you see that boat story on Disney Sunday night?"

"That big raft thing or whatever it was?"

"Yea. That would be so fun to sail on the ocean like that."

"We don't have an ocean."

"We don't need one. We can use a beaver dam."

"What are you going to use for a boat?" Bill asked.

"We can build one."

"Out of what?"

"Remember that big junk pile behind your dad's maintenance shed?"

"Yea."

"We could use some of those old barrels to make a boat."

"Let's go look," Bill said as he downed his last gulp of pop. "Kill it," he told his friend as he stood up and turned the knob on the door.

He tipped his bottle skyward and drank the rest of his pop, his Adam's apple sliding up and down with each gulp. After the last gulp was gone, he handed his buddy the empty bottle and stood up. Bill opened the door and placed the two empty bottles in the wooden bottle case, making sure Faulk noticed that he did.

Bill's dad owner a large road building firm. The maintenance garage was located in the middle of town and most of the maintenance on these big Caterpillar® machines was done over the winter. During the summer, the machines were gone and the big lot and maintenance building stood quiet and empty. There were discarded old bulldozer parts, barrels, and heavy steel mesh used to reinforce roads.

"See those barrels," he said as he pointed at two barrels on the big scrap pile. "And that piece of metal mesh," he said as he pointed to another item on the junk heap. "If we put those barrels under that mesh, we'll have a pontoon boat."

Bill's eyes got bigger as the idea and the potential adventure came to life from the pile of junk.

"How will we attached the barrels to the mesh?" he asked.

"Rope," his friend answered. "We'll tie them on."

"Rope will rot in the water," bill answered, "we'll need to weld the barrels to the mesh."

"But Art is out on the road," his friend said as he pointed out that Bill's dad's do-it-all foreman, who would likely help them, was out with the road building crew.

"I'll get my mom to do it," Bill said. "She knows how to weld."

Bill knew his mom would go along with almost anything that was educational and fun for the kids. The two boys had all of the necessary parts for their dream boat set up right next to the junk pile. All they had to do was sell her on the idea of coming down to the lot and have a look at the project.

Bill knew his mom well. Even though the house was only a few minutes away from the maintenance lot, he knew his mom was not one to stay in the same place for a long time. She was not one to engineer the idea. She was not one to crawl around in an oily scrap iron pile. But, if everything was in place, she was one to go along with the idea.

They climbed up in the big scrap pile and retrieved the mesh and the barrels and setup the boat of their dreams below the pile. They already knew where to find a couple of stout poles to help them navigate the creek, so if construction could be pushed up a little, they could go from scrap pile to water by the morning Nebraska tide.

"Mom," Bill blurted out as he stood behind her in the family kitchen with just a touch or two of grease on his white T-shirt, "can you help us finish our boat?"

"Why sure," she said as she turned from the sink, wiped her hands briskly on a kitchen towel and looked toward the table expecting to see a partially completed plastic model of a navy destroyer sitting on the living room table. "Where is it?"

"It's down at the lot," he continued as his voice increased in urgency. "It's a special project that we are working on, Mom, and it won't take but a few minutes to put together. Won't you come down to the lot with us. Please?"

"Do you mean a real boat?" she asked her son who was now following her around the kitchen as she put away the newly washed pots, pans, and dishes.

"Yabut Mom this is a special boat that will allow us to do research and stuff."

"Research?"

"Yea, for school and scouts," he continued. "It will help us learn about fish and wildlife and trees."

"All right," she said, "let's go take a look at this boat."

The adopted engineer and two budding sailors walked the short block to the back of the maintenance shop where the boat project sat. She carefully surveyed the project.

"Where did you find these barrels?" she asked.

"They were in the scrap pile out back along with this piece of mesh."

"You're sure they were in the scrap pile," she said as she looked at the two boys and double-checked their facial expressions for an honest answer.

"Positive," came the quick response from her son.

"This stuff will have to be welded together and I don't think Art is in town," she said as she turned around and headed for home. "You'll probably have to wait until Art gets back."

"Mom, you can do it," her son pleaded. "You can use the welder in the shop. I know you can do it, please Mom."

"Well maybe this evening but we'll have to get everything into the shop in order to use the welder." She couldn't pass up this adventure and considering the depth of Bow Creek, there was a greater threat from mosquito bites than there was from high seas and drowning.

There was another major problem. The boat was outside and the welder was inside and there was a locked door between them and she didn't have a key. The big shop door could be opened from the inside. It was starting to look like a "maybe tomorrow" and the boys knew that a "maybe tomorrow" sometimes never comes. She was already several yard ahead of the boys when they turned back to their dream project and the locked shop door that was between them and their adventurous dream.

Bill carefully eyed the building and found a window, a very small one high in the back wall of the shop building, right above the giant scrap pile. It was propped open with a small stick.

"If you can boost me to that window up there, " he said as he pointed out the small window twenty feet above them at the top of the scrap pile, I can probably get in and open the big door."

"That's breaking and entering."

"No it's not," Bill said. "It's my dad's company."

With a barrel and a boost from his shorter and fatter friend, Bill managed to get a good grip on the small window ledge and slither through the window. The friend listened to Bill's shoes struggle and crash against the inside wall. Then silence.

"Ooof," he heard from inside the building. The friend suddenly realized getting through the window wasn't the problem—getting down to the floor inside was the problem, especially in a dark building.

"Hey! Are you OK?"

He worried about his friend inside. What if he fell and was hurt? What should he do? What would Bill's mom say? What would his mom say? The consequences of guilty actions raced through his mind.

Finally the agonizing silence ended as he heard noise coming from the front of the building. He ran to the front of the building and a smile started to come over his face as giant front doors of the machine shop slowly started to open and a ray of light hit his greasy friend's smiling face. They were in the boat building business.

Inside the big shop was everything a ship builder needed. Welder. Welder's helmet. Heavy gloves. Welding rods of all types. Big c-clamps to hold everything together. There was a giant overhead chain driven hoist to load the ship onto the company truck, which was parked right inside of the door.

"Let's get the stuff," Bill said to his friend as he dashed out of the darkness toward the barrels and mesh. In a few minutes, the boys had their boat sitting right next to the welder.

"Mom won't lollygag around but if everything is in place, she'll do it."

"Maybe after dinner," she said as they stood in the kitchen pleading their case again.

"Well for someone, who had nothing to do, you sure managed to stay busy all day," his mother said as he came through the back door of his house.

"What's is all of that grease on your clothes," his mother asked as the boy tried to slip by her notice and take his place at the dinner table.

"You aren't going to eat until you get those hands washed! What were you doing today? You and Bill are building what? Does Bill's mother know about this? Where do you plan to put this boat? That could be dangerous. You could drown," his mother's endless list of questions continued as the rest of the family took their places at the dinner table.

"I don't like this idea one bit," she said as she forgot the grease and started serving the family dinner. His brothers teased him. His father listened. The boy got up and started for the back room and the comfort of the dog.

"Come back here and finish your dinner or you're not going anywhere, mister!"

"But Mom, you told me to create my own adventures."

"You'll have to get your father's permission before you go off on any boating expedition—especially in a home-made boat. I can't believe Bill's mom would go along with such and idea."

His chance at his big dream seemed as doomed. He looked at his dad. No chance, he thought.

"I think it's a good idea," his dad said. "Wear a life jacket."

He grinned from ear to ear as he jumped up and carried his dirty dishes to the sink.

"Can I be excused?" he asked.

"Yes," his mother said. She was clearly irritated.

He was out the door as fast as a longshoremen when the shift whistle blows. He assumed Bill would be ready and his mom would be sold and ready to put hand to welder. He found his friend doing dishes and his mother was talking to and feeding a variety of pets.

Rather than wait for his friend to finish his chores, he pitched in and helped. In the less than twenty minutes, Bill's mom was leaning over mesh and barrels, complete with helmet and gloves, guiding the welding rod across the bow and stern of one of the neatest boats Hartington, Nebraska would ever see.

When she finished her assembly task and when the shop had been properly cleaned up and tools put back in their proper places, the boys moved their new boat. With the aid of the big hoist and few chains, the easiest part of the project was done. Their boat was loaded into a company pickup and ready to be launched the following morning.

Bow Creek is a fairly fast moving stream but not more than a couple of inches deep. It couldn't float a branch in most spots let alone float this boat.

"Look at the trees by the creek as we drive along," she ordered. "If you see some limbs on the ground or short stumps that come to a sharp point, sing out."

She wanted them to look for signs of muskrats and beavers. All they had to do is find a beaver dam and a farmer who wouldn't mind water-squatters. All of those conditions had to be close to a road. The boat was too heavy for two kids and one mom to do anything more than slide it down the two boards they brought along and into the creek. They criss-crossed Bow Creek for about an hour and finally found just the right spot.

After they had the permission of the farmer, she backed the truck off the road, through the ditch, through the gate and down to water's edge. She got out and dropped the tailgate. The boys and the mom dragged the ship out of the back of the truck, pushed it down the bank, through the nettles, through the black sticky fly infested mud, and into the beaver-made lake. Finally, their dream boat was afloat.

"Look at that," Bill said as the ripples from their boat slipped across the still water. They watched as it started to float with the current.

"That's neat," his friend said. "That is really neat."

The little beaver-made lake was three feet deep and only the bottom quarter of the barrels were actually submerged in the water. Their big summer dream had come true. The beaver lake was seventy feet long but it was enough for their summer needs.

"Now you boys be careful," Bill's mom said as she looked down from the bank at the barrels she had crafted into a sturdy boat. "I'll be back in a few hours to get you."

"We will," Bill's friend hollered back as he waded out into the water and pulled himself up on the boat's mesh deck. "Thanks," he said as he smiled and waved back to her.

They spent the rest of the day sailing their beaver-made sea and living their summer dream. They watched as the muskrats poked their heads out of the water to see who was invading their lake. The watched a hawk swooped down from the sky as an unsuspecting field mouse became dinner for the hawk. They looked into the water and saw the minnows swimming along side their boat when the water was calm and dart away when they broke the glass-like stillness with their poles.

They sailed themselves sleepy and they dreamed of sailing the world as thunderstorms pelted the area with hail and heavy rains that night. Along with the heavy rains came a flash flood on Bow Creek. The beaver dam was swept away. The gangplank was swept away. And, worst of all, their prize boat was swept away.

"It's gone," Bill said as he looked at the tall weeds now smashed flat against the bank. They could see the ravages of the flash flood; a wall of water eight feet high had swept down Bow Creek taking everything with it.

"What does Art use that big engine for that is in the corner of the machine shop?" Bill's friend asked as they walked down the road.

"I don't know? Why?"

"Think we could build a race car?"

Niobrara Summer

———————— ◆ ————————

"Hey, wait up!" Jack hollered out as he recognized his buddy from a block away.

His bike slid sideways, killing his built-up speed as he reached his waiting buddy.

"Did you hear?" Jack asked. "We're going next week."

"Really?" his friend answered as a big smile crossed his face. "Got any money for hooks and weights?"

It was the middle of August and the days of summer finally settled in. Tornado season has pretty much subsided and the restless air of spring has given way to sultry stillness. This is corn-growing weather in Nebraska. Hot humid and still.

The air was still all over Nebraska. It just didn't move because it was so heavy with Gulf moisture. As soon as the sun was high enough in the sky, beads of sweat started forming and fresh clothes soon became wet towels sticking to clammy skin.

It was uncomfortable enough to require a change of scene because this kind of uncomfortable living kept tempers on edge. This was a great time to take a split vacation, mom and kids out of town, dog and dad stayed home.

"Are we going to Niobrara?" he asked Jack, still puffing from the bike ride.

"Yup, but my sisters are going, too."

"Ah darn, they'll screw everything up. What about a boat?"

"I think I can talk my mom into one. I got my lifesaving merit badge this year you know."

"Not me, I can't swim ten feet."

Niobrara is a small town with just a few hundred people in the Northeast part of Nebraska. The town was built just to the west of the Santee Sioux reservation and near where the Niobrara River joined the mighty Missouri. Custer roamed this area on his way to a date with the Ogallala nation, the mighty cousins of the Santee.

The week passed with anxious agony as the boys planned the details of their week at Niobrara State Park.

Niobrara was the vacation away from the big city. No Ladies Day at the golf club. No bridge club. No traffic hassles from the town of 1,500 people.

The Niobrara River must have gotten lost in the early days because it's natural beauty belonged in a Montana or Wyoming setting rather than the rolling, almost desert like part of Nebraska called the Sand Hills.

"Think we'll need any of these?" Jack asked as they examined each fishing hook, lure, bobber and weight in the Coast to Coast® hardware store.

"Get the big hooks. I am going to catch him this year."

"He won't be there," Jack answered. "Somebody must have caught him by now."

"He's still there. If anyone would have caught him, it would have been in the Cedar County News."

By mid-afternoon, they were standing on the banks of the lagoon, which winded through the park just in front of the 1920's style wooden cabins. The lagoon came off of the river, but without much water movement, it was taken over by water plants and moss.

"Be careful around that lagoon," Jack's mother cautioned. "If you fall in with all of that moss, you could get tangled up and drown. Don't go near it without a life jacket."

"Awe Mom," Jack protested.

"No awe mom. That's an order. No life jacket. No fishing. The bank is too steep. One slip and you will be in that water and moss."

Even the green moss covered lagoon offered some relief for those who were not patient enough to wait for the swimming pool to open, but they had to be out of sight of the mothers and not in the worst mossy areas. The lagoon was up to ten feet deep, twenty feet wide and the banks were steep. They could fish from small docks in front of each cabin or from a crossing bridge but they wanted to rent a rowboat.

They were spending a week at the park. Jack, his mom and two sisters in one cabin. His friend, his mom and one brother in the neighboring cabin. They lived on grilled hot dogs, hamburgers, bacon and eggs, and Spagetteos® for the impatient.

"What's the deal on the boat?"

"I asked but they are not too keen on the idea," Jack said. "Your mom is worried about the moss and some kid drowned here last year."

"Don't worry. I'll talk her into it."

By nightfall, the families were settled in and enjoying their first night at the park. His mom was having a glass of ice tea on the screened porch. She looked relaxed and he knew it was now or never.

"Mom, Jack and I need a rowboat so we can catch that big fish in the lagoon."

"You can't swim and there is all kinds of moss and stuff in there. If you fell out of the boat, you could drown. I am not in favor of the boat idea."

"But Mom, how can we fish then?"

"You could fish off the bridge."

"But Mom, that big fish is to smart to be close to that bridge. It's too noisy and he'll swim away when something goes over the bridge. Plus, somebody might be a bad driver and hit us. We need a boat. Please Mom?"

"Then you have to promise me that you will wear a lifejacket all the time and that you won't go near the river opening."

"I will. We won't."

"I mean it. You violate those rules and the boat goes back instantly."

"We won't."

If the fishing was good, the families feasted on bullheads barely over the legal limit and fresh from the Nebraska Game and Parks stocking truck. All the boys had to do was row the boat down to the bridge where the stocking truck was dumping the fish into the lagoon. They were so hungry they would bite on an empty hook.

They learned how to catch bullfrogs with a piece of red cloth on a fishing hook. They learned what frog's legs tasted like from other folks in the park since both of these mothers had no interest in cooking froglegs.

"They taste kinda like chicken," Jack told his mom as he got back from the frog leg fry at the neighbor's cabin.

"I would rather have the chicken."

"Really Mom," Jack said, "they are pretty good."

"Would you rather have the frog legs or my fried chicken?" she said as she turned away from making a bed and looked at her son.

"Your friend chicken."

"Smart boy," she said. "Now help me make this bed up since you will be sleeping in it."

The cabin had everything a family needed, at least for a cramped week. Bunk beds. A gas stove and small refrigerator. It had big windows. They needed big windows at night to try and get the air moving. And, most important, a screened porch. Without the screens, they were the bait as the sky filled with the plague of summer—mosquitoes. The still lagoon was mosquito-growing country. The pools of water from the spring rains and floods from the Niobrara and the nearby Missouri were the perfect breeding grounds for the plague that infested paradise.

But, the mosquitoes were badly needed. They were food. Fish food. And you could hear the fish jumping all night long for their dinner including him.

He was the big one. He was there every summer and teased the boys with bites on their lines and loud splashes when he jumped in the middle of the night.

Those splashes sounded like someone threw a big rock in the water when he jumped. But it wasn't a rock. It was him. He was the one that hit your bait and left your hook empty—the one that made a red and white bobber, even the big one, send out tidal waves before it disappeared into the green murkey moss below. You gave your biggest yank but he was already eating your bait and gone while your hook flew over your head into a patch of nettles on the bank. The fisherman had to choose to get itchy or cut the line. They changed to bigger hooks and bobbers. He changed to bigger bites.

"Did you hear him jump last night?" Jack asked. "I almost jumped out of bed and grabbed my pole and went after him."

Toward the end of the week, they had our fill of catching six-inch bullheads. They weren't interested in fish that just bobbed at the end of the pole. They wanted the bamboo breaker, a chance at the fish that could bend the pole into a loupe and break it as you fought back. They wanted him in their world. He was tough enough to stay in his. Something had to give.

"Come on fish. Break the pole," he said as he cast out his line, big hook and bobber, took off his life jacket and sat down in the boat to wait for his prize fish to come and play.

This bass was big enough to feed almost everyone in the two cabins but the boys had other plans for him. They would take a picture holding him being mindful that even out of the water and near death, this giant bass still had the power to spring back to freedom. He belonged on a plaque on a big office wall. But all week long, this king of the lagoon had other plans. He stayed pat in his lagoon. The hell with visitors. The boy's eyes got as big as silver dollars when he jumped. He was a record fish.

"Think we could get our picture in the Cedar County News if we caught him?" Jack asked.

"Without a doubt. Plus, we would be the topic of conversation at the Cedar Café, too. We would be heroes."

Just at that instant, the big fish jumped out of the water only ten feet from the boat. Jack watched as his friend jumped to his feet as the big bass made a run at his line. The bobber disappeared from the surface as if it were a rock falling through the air. He yanked his pole over his shoulder as the line snapped tight. The bamboo pole went from straight to forming a curve as it snapped and turned in his hands. The boat rocked as he fought the fish, leaning backward and forward in the boat and then suddenly, he fell overboard and disappeared in the big splash into the moss below.

"Hey!" Jack cried out as he grabbed at his friend as he went over the side of the boat. He knew he couldn't swim and as soon as they were out of view of the cabin, he had taken off his life vest.

Jack took off his life vest and prepared to jump in after his friend.

"No! No! Stop! Don't go in there without a life jacket!" he heard his mother screaming as she and his friend's mom came running toward them.

Then the water splashed again as his friend stood up, coughing and spitting water out of his mouth. He was covered with green moss and other water plants. and standing in waist deep water, his pole snapped at mid length, and no fish on his line.

"Missed him, dammit," he said as he walked to the shore pulling the boat and his friend with him. "I almost had him."

"Take that boat back this instant," his mother order. "And then get back here, clean up, and get packed. We're leaving."

Their week was over. The cabin was clean and ready for a new family. The boat was back at the rental house and the boys were in the car ready to go. As they followed Jack's family car across the bridge over the moss covered green lagoon, he saw a streak of silver jump out of the water and make a big loop and a splash back into the lagoon.

"Goodbye big fish," he said. "This year you're better than me."

The Eagle
Who Couldn't Swim

$\blacklozenge$

He was starting to change in a lot of ways. He was already counting the months until he could get his driver's license. He was interested in sports and girls looked much different than they used to look. Besides not being old enough for cars, sports, and in some parent's minds, girls, his big problem was boredom.

"Are you going to Camp Cedars this year?" his friend Jim asked him as they put away the flags used at the scout meeting.

"I don't know," he answered. "I don't know if I am going to stay in scouts much longer."

"Really? Why not?"

"It's not that much fun anymore. We just do the same stuff."

"Camp Cedars will be fun this year," his buddy pointed out. "I bet we both will get in Order of the Arrow and I will get the two merit badges I need to qualify for eagle."

"Eagle? You are that close to eagle?"

"Yup. Three more merit badges. Lifesaving canoeing and signaling."

"I have a bunch of them left plus I can't swim so there will be no Eagle Scout in my family."

"I bet you will get into Order of the Arrow," his friend said.

"You think so?"

"I know so but you won't ever know unless you go to camp."

"Well, maybe I'll go then."

He had been a good scout and had earned everything but Eagle Scout. His fellow scouts and leaders could vote him into the honor society of scouting, The Order of the Arrow, but that only happened at summer camp. To get in the order, he had to go to camp.

Scouting went from nothing to a very big something because of a man who decided he would turn an ordinary program into an extraordinary program. He loved the outdoors and since he worked for the United States Soil Conservation Service, he was a man of the land. He knew there were enough boys in this small town who were standing in line just waiting for the chance to learn.

"All right, listen up," the scoutmaster said as he put the three fingers and the crossed thumb scout salute into the air above his head to indicate order and silence, "if you are going to Camp Cedars, you need to sign up tonight."

"Go on, sign up," his friend said. "We'll have a great time."

"Maybe," the boy said, "I'm just not sure I am going to stay in scouting."

Before long, all of the folding chairs were folded and put away. The flags, heavy with award ribbons won by Troop 173, were back in the storage closet. Some of the boys were already gone and the rest were close to leaving.

"I don't see your name on the Camp Cedars list?" the scoutmaster said to him as he was getting ready to leave.

"I may not be going."

"Can I ask why?" said the scoutmaster, "you have always been there to help us and this is your year to qualify for Order of the Arrow."

"I know," the boy said as he searched for the right words to tell this man he respected so much that he was no longer that interested in scouting. "I guess it's just not that much fun for me anymore."

"Well, we need to have a little talk. Can you stay a couple of minutes?"

"My ride will be here soon."

"That's OK, let's just talk about a couple of things."

"OK."

"I know there are other things that are starting to interest you and I know you have some doubts about making the eagle rank because of swimming and lifesaving," the scoutmaster said. "This is probably your last year in scouting and I want you to enjoy it and remember it."

"But if I can't swim, I will never make eagle."

"If you don't try, you won't know what the eagle award really means, will you?"

"No. I suppose I won't."

"Not everything you do is going to be handed to you. Some things you will never get but that doesn't mean you shouldn't try," the scout-master said. "Those are often the things that will make you much smarter and wiser. In a lot of ways, life is like swimming. You must reach out and pull yourself through the water to swim well. You must reach out and pull yourself through life, too. Understand?'

"Yes, I think so."

"I would love to see you become an Eagle Scout but I would hate to see you not try to become one. Please reconsider your decision to go to camp."

"OK."

"Good," the scoutmaster said as he patted the boy on the shoulder. "Looks like your ride is here. Call me when you know."

"OK. Good night."

He thought about what the scoutmaster told him. He knew he would have to qualify this year or not at all. He thought about failure. He thought about the idea of not trying. He wondered which would be worse.

He needed three merit badges to qualify for eagle—swimming, life saving, and canoeing. Each of those merit badges built on skills learned from the prior one. Swimming skills were necessary for the life saving merit badge. Life saving skills were necessary for the canoeing merit badge. After all, if you dumped a canoe full of people and somebody in the canoe couldn't swim, it would be nice if somebody could pull that person to safety, wouldn't it? He couldn't swim worth a darn—polio had left him with one arm shorter and weaker than the other. He couldn't control his arm well enough to coordinate the necessary strokes and swim the required distances. Boy Scouts built his values. Swimming killed his confidence. It stood between him and the highest scouting award.

There was nothing he wanted more than to become an Eagle Scout. He would be one of the first three boys in the community to reach that goal. The town was already buzzing about which boy would be first. Mothers asked other mothers if their boy was going to make the Eagle Scout rank. Fathers beamed. There was as much community interest in the competition to be first as there was in any of the sports at the local schools. Even though he was a dark horse to be first, most folks thought he certainly would be one of the first. He felt the eyes of the town. He had heard more "you can do it" praise from family, friends of family, and even ordinary neighbors.

Deep in his heart, he knew he just couldn't quit. It was better to try and maybe fail than to not try at all.

"I have decided to go to camp," he said to the scoutmaster through the phone.

"Good," the scoutmaster said. "I need your help this year. You can help me get the new boys off to a good start in scouting."

He was surprised by what the scoutmaster said. He had never thought of himself as useful to the scoutmaster. He never thought he could teach younger scouts anything.

"You'll be senior patrol leader for this camp, OK?"

"Ya. Sure," the boy said. "If that's what you want."

"That's what I want. I want my best scout to help me out."

Scouting is based on many things but advancement through newly acquired skills is the cornerstone. Boys started with the tenderfoot rank which was within fairly easy reach—tie a few knots the right way and some dear sweet mom could put her sewing skills to work on the left breast pocket of the khaki shirt by sewing the tenderfoot patch in place. Next in line was the second class rank—a little more challenging. Next was the first class rank—the young lad should be qualified to stay in the woods overnight and if he accidentally hit himself in the leg with his trusty scout ax, he could stop the bleeding by himself. The top prize of scouting was just above first class—eagle.

He had been to five summer camps, a jamboree, and dozens of camp-outs in all types of weather, including a winter camp-out in below zero weather. He knew what it was like to hike twenty miles with a pack. He had a lot of things that he could teach new scouts. His sash was full of merit badges and he could offer lots of insight to young scouts interested in everything from astronomy to zoology.

Camp was an exercise in organization. The right boys had to be at the right activities at the right time. He knew all of the rights at Camp Cedars because he had been through all of them. He could make sure the young scouts had good memories, too.

"Bet you didn't know there was so much planning involved in this," the scoutmaster said as he sat down at a camp picnic table with his senior patrol leader. "I am taking most of the older boys to the advance swimming class at nine and I want you to take the new kids on a little hike down by the river. Show them some of the plants and trees down there. Can you do that?"

"Sure," the boy said. "How far do you want me to take them? Ten or fifteen miles?"

"Oh no," the scoutmaster said as he laughed and picked up his clipboard and got up from the table, "take them on an hour hike—a couple of miles or so. That's plenty."

"All right," the scoutmaster said as he put the familiar scout quiet sign in the air, "listen up." The boys gathered quickly in front of their various patrol flags. Beaver Patrol. Buffalo Patrol. Mountain Lion Patrol. Elk Patrol.

"Tenderfoot scouts go with the senior patrol leader on a nature hike this morning. The rest of you are with me. Let's get organized."

The scouts scurried in and out of their tents and were soon formed into two groups and heading down two different trails in two different directions. Camp Cedars was coming alive with scouts and with everything nature had to offer on a summer Nebraska afternoon.

"Where is Anderson?" the new senior patrol leader asked the ten young boys following in his footsteps on a dirt trail hacked through the underbrush along Nebraska's Platte River.

"The last time I saw him was when we first reached the river," one of the young scouts said. They huddled around him and looked scared.

"Should we spread out and try to find him?" one of the young scouts asked. "Did he fall in the river and drown?"

"Let's not get worried. It's times like these when you need to be calm. He can't be far behind so I am going to go back and check," he told the boys.

"What should we do?" another boy asked.

"All of you guys stay right here," he ordered. "I'll be back in a couple of minutes. See if you can pick out three different trees while I am gone. You all stay together. No exceptions. I want you to be able to identify three types of trees by the time I get back."

The boys sat down as ordered and started to look at the different trees, which towered above them. He watched to make sure they would follow his orders before he started to look for the missing boy. He was clearly anxious and worried about the boy but he knew he shouldn't show his worry to the remaining boys.

"Be right back. Don't worry," he said as he started slowly back down the trail. As he got further away from the boys, he increased his speed.

He knew he needed to stay calm, too. He carefully retraced the steps of his young khaki-clad army; he read the signs—the footprints, the branches, the trampled weeds. Finally he spotted the missing scout in a patch of weeds.

"I wouldn't use those leaves to wipe with," he said to the missing and now very surprised scout. "That's poison ivy."

"Any problems on your hike?" the scoutmaster asked as the he returned with his young band of tree smart rookies.

"Nope. Got one case of poison ivy," he answered.

"Can you take him up to the first aid center?"

"Sure."

"Take your swim suit with you. Your swimming trials are in a half hour."

"OK."

"You can take the young guys on a horse ride at two this afternoon, OK?"

"That will be great."

"Flag ceremony and dinner at five," the scoutmaster said as he looked as his agenda. "Have them shower and get dressed in uniform for that. I want us to look sharp at this camp."

"Will do."

He liked his new role and the scoutmaster liked him in that role. He was away from the teen pressure he was feeling at home and having a good time helping out. He was good at following orders and helping the younger boys learn about nature and scouting. But, he still had to swim.

"OK, listen up," the camp swimming instructor said as the older scouts trying for the swimming merit badge sat on the edge of the pool. "Today we want to get an idea of your swimming ability so we can classify you and put you into appropriate groups for training. We will ask you, four at a time, to jump in at that end of the pool and swim to the other end of the pool. Use a regular breaststroke. OK, line up in four lines."

The lines formed quickly. He was last in line and there would only be two other guys in his group. He noticed some of his young scouts standing behind the fence watching him. "Damn," he thought, "they can all swim better than me."

"Ready?" the instructor asked as the first group of four boys stood at the edge of the pool, "go."

Other groups followed quickly. The calm pool turned into thrashing waves as healthy young boys dove in one end of the Olympic pool and soon popped out of the other end. He grew more anxious as he advanced, only a foot at a time, toward the edge of the pool. The crowd in front of him slowly disappeared until he stood with the last boys in line, starring at the empty thrashing blue water surrounded by dozens of other boys who had already survived this test of courage. What was fun for them, became pure living Boy Scout hell for him.

"Go," he heard the instructor holler out.

With the other two boys, he dove into the water and threw his right arm out ahead, cupped his hand and pulled back. He started kicking his feet as he brought his left arm out of the water, tried to cup his hand and thrashed it down almost straight out from his left side. His timing was gone as he came to a full stop, gulped down a mouthful of water and gasped for air.

He didn't have a problem on the right side of his body. His strong right arm could reach out and cut through the water and produce the power to pull him through the water. It was his left side. His left arm was smaller and weaker. He couldn't control his movements with the same exact control. The muscles were not there. They had been destroyed. His hand was different, too. It had been rebuilt by surgery but it wasn't perfect. He couldn't form the necessary pulling cup to pull him through the water. He was a rock in a pool full of fish.

"Hey, that guy keeps bumping into me!" the scout to his left protested.

No amount of counselor psychology, mental imaging, or guts could make his left arm do what it had to do to help him become an Eagle Scout. He couldn't swim well enough.

The instructor could see he was in trouble and jumped in after him. He grabbed him around the chest and pulled him to the side. The two other boys swam on. With the help of two other instructors, they pulled him from the pool. He pushed them away and walked into the bathhouse and away from the pool toward the campsite. He said nothing. He never looked back.

His young bunch of scouts followed him. They said nothing. They were confused, not sure what had happened or what they should say. He wasn't aware of them until he reached his tent and heard them stop behind him. He turned and looked at them.

"You guys take showers and be in full uniform in ten minutes."

They looked at his angry eyes and scrambled to obey his orders. He fulfilled his duties the rest of the week but never returned to that swimming pool.

On Thursday night, he stepped out of his tent in full uniform. He wore a sash of merit badges, four across, that started by his right shoulder and went to the bottom of the shash at his left waistline. His first class patch was on his left pocket. His jamboree patch was on his left sleeve and under that was his rank of senior patrol leader. He didn't notice the young scouts who noticed him. They looked at all of the color, all of the awards, and wondered if someday they would look the same.

"OK, listen up," the scoutmaster said. "Tonight is the tapping out ceremony for the Order of the Arrow. The scouts selected in this tapping out ceremony are the best scout at this camp and we might just have one or two of them right here."

The young bunch switched their attention from the scoutmaster to their senior patrol leader. Would he get in they wondered? What would it be like? But, he couldn't swim, would he still get in? Could you be one of the best scouts and not be able to swim?

"Tapped" was a nice word for what would happen. All of the scouts at camp stood in a big circle around this giant bonfire. The older scouts, who were member of the Order, were dressed in the costume of the Great Plains Indians, circled slowly outside of the big circle. In the center of the circle, in front of the roaring bonfire, stood the leaders of the Order who called out the names of those scouts which had been nominated by his peers, his leaders, and the counselors at camp. When a name was called, the boy stepped forward from his circle of friends. The boy was then rushed from behind by Indian-dressed scouts and dragged to the center of the circle. The tap was like a blind-side hit from an All-American linebacker. The newly tapped scouts were hustled off to the woods and not allowed to see their hometown buddies for the rest of the night.

These newly tapped scouts were allowed to take a sleeping bag with them. They were lead blindfolded through the dark night and the dark woods to an unknown campground. Unlike the other campsites at summer camp, this site didn't have any tents constructed on the top of deck-like board structures. This campsite was just as God had made it—brush, trees, nettles, and vines down by the Platte River where an attack squadron of hungry mosquitoes lay in wait.

The boys had to create a campsite in that mess and get a good night's sleep. They were not allowed to speak for the entire night and the next day. Not one word. During the night, each scout had to carve a wooden arrow, complete with his name and troop number on it. That arrow had to be with that nominated scout at all times. Other members of the Order could ask to see that arrow anytime they wanted to see it. If the scout said something and got caught talking by an Order member, that member could carve a notch in the scout's arrow. Three notches and the scout was out.

He took his knife and started to cut branches and weeds to create bedding for the night. Off in the distance, he could see lightning and hear thunder as a squall line moved toward Camp Cedars. Chances were good for a Nebraska thunderstorm and torrential rain. He built a lean-too from a bunch of small branches and weaved some big leaves into the structure to try and keep the driving rain off of his face. With a leave covering over his sleeping bag and the lean-too, there was a slim chance for spending part of the night dry. He stuffed some dry twigs and snapped some dry branches into small pieces and put them under his sleeping bag under the learn-too. He found some dry grass to put over the sticks. When the sleeping bag was placed back over the little pile of dry sticks and grass, he had a pillow and maybe, enough dry material to start a small fire in the morning.

As part of his challenge, he and all of the other candidates were given a raw egg for breakfast. If they could create a fire, and could figure out a way to cook the egg without a pan, they could have a cooked egg for breakfast. Of course they could not use any matches to build that egg cooking fire. They could rub sticks together, or strike rocks together, but absolutely no matches. His pillow could be very useful when morning came.

He tossed and turned and flinched with each bolt of lightning as the storms moved overhead. The heavy driving rains came and his lean-too kept most of the rain off of him. He could hear the other scouts moving around as morning neared.

Another scout screamed as he woke up with a snake soundly sleeping on his somewhat dry warm stomach.

"It's a bull snake not a rattler," the boy said to his scared-stiff friend. He looked around to see if any of the Order members were around and listening.

Several scouts tried to start fires rubbing sticks together and hit various types of rock together without success. He brought out his pillow, found a dry place where a sleeping bag used to be, and used two dry sticks to create a fire. As he rubbed the sticks together, his friends fed dry grass against the ends of the sticks until a small column of smoke started to rise. He gently blew on the new ember until a flame popped through the dry grass. He tended the fire like it was a baby trying to live. Soon the fire burned and as the fire burned, he pulled coals from it, wrapped his egg in a big wet leaf, and covered it with more coals. He would have a hard-boiled egg for breakfast, and as he shared his fire, so would his silent buddies.

Twenty-four hours later, he watched as his arrow with one notch was nailed to the rafters of the camp dining room. He was a full-fledged member of Order of the Arrow.

On the last day of camp, he stood quietly and looked through the chain link fence at the camp pool. There wasn't a ripple in the aqua-blue water. He could see the lane lines painted in dark blue on the bottom of the pool. On the clear surface were the ropes with the blue and white markers that separated the lanes on top of the water. He knew he would never be an Eagle Scout. He had come face-to-face with his first major defeat but in the minds of many, he would always be the Eagle Scout who couldn't swim.

"It took courage for you to jump in there with those other guys you know," his scoutmaster said as he walked up and put his hand on the boy's shoulder. "I would rather be known for my courage any day."

"Thanks," he said as he smiled at his scoutmaster. "I am glad I came. I am glad I made the Order."

"You will always be one the best," his scoutmaster said. "Just stay away from water," he said as he smiled and messed up the teenager's blond hair.

The boy laughed as he turned away from the pool and headed for the parking lot.

"OK, listen up," the scoutmaster hollered out, "let's go home."

Black Snow

———————— ◆ ————————

"The sheriff has a young black kid in jail," he said as he came though the back door of the house and started to relay the news of the day to his wife and boy now headed for the dinner table.

"What has he done to be put in jail?" his wife started to question. "How old is he? Does the sheriff know where he's from or who his parents are? His poor mothers must be worried sick," she continued as she served dinner.

"He found him half dead and locked in a semi truck trailer full of oyster shells down at the Laurel weigh station. Apparently he decided to run away from home and sneaked into the back of this truck."

"In a truck load of oyster shells!" she said. "It's freezing outside! How could he have possibly kept warm in a truck trailer? And, it would be pitch dark in there. How long was he in that truck? What kind of food and care could he possibly get in that old jail. For God sake, that is no place for a lost boy! Mercy, mercy."

She worried about old neighbors when the weather was bad. She worried when a friend had a doctor's appointment. She worried about skinny stray cats. But when it came to a young boy, she really worried. She knew the fear and worries that only a mother could know.

"The sheriff is trying to make contact with his parents right now through the authorities in Alabama. He'll stay in jail until they find them," the husband said as he started to eat his fried chicken.

"The jail is no place for him," she said as she sat down at the family table with her husband and her very quiet son. "He could just as well stay here until his parents can come and get them," she suggested.

"We already have a knothead," the husband said as he looked up and smiled at his son. "Besides, we don't know anything about him and his story may not be true."

"How old is he?" she asked.

"Thirteen."

"That's much too young to be locked up in that old drafty jail in the middle of winter."

"He isn't locked up," he said. "The door is open and I'm sure the sheriff's wife is feeding him properly. I am sure he will be comfortable while he is here. As soon as the sheriff finds his parents, he'll be on their way home."

"Dad, why are they bringing oyster shells up here?"

"Farmers use them for chicken feed," his dad answered.

"Did the sheriff arrest him because he was a stow-a-way?"

"He didn't arrest him," his dad continued. "He brought him here for his safety. If they hadn't found him, he might have frozen to death."

The small town grapevine was red hot. The phone started to ring as dinner was coming to an end.

"Mom, it's for you," her son said as he held out the phone.

"Hello?" she said as she held the receiver to her ear, put her hand on her hip, and looked off in a distant stare. "Yes!" she said, "we were just talking about that. I feel so bad that he's up in that old drafty jail. That's a terrible place for young boy."

"Ah ha. Um. Oh he did. Oh you are. That's wonderful. Why sure he will," she said as her distant glance suddenly focused on her son.

Something was up he thought as he eyed the aluminum pie tin which still had a remaining piece of apple pie in it. His father retired to the family room and the television set as she hung up the phone.

"That was Blanch Rahn," she said to her husband as he looked up from his newspaper reading. "The boy is out of jail and are staying with John and Blanch. He'll stay with the Rahns until the sheriff could locate the his family."

"That's a good idea," he said as he continued his paper reading. "The kid couldn't be in a better place that that. He will want for nothing if John has anything to say about it."

"And Blanch wanted to know if you could go over to their house and spend some time with him," she said as she patted her son on the shoulder.

"That's a good idea, too," his father said as he turned the next page of the paper.

"Ahbut Dad!"

"You're going."

"Ahbut Dad, I have too much homework," he pleaded

"You've suddenly become a serious student?"

"But Dad, I don't know nothing about this kid. He could be a killer or something."

"Didn't they teach you how to defend yourself in scouts?" his father asked as he put down the paper. "And let's not forget who is asking you to his house. This is the same Mr. Rahn who took you fishing at Lewis and Clark Lake a few times last year. Do you want him to think you are no longer Mr. Terrific?"

The boy let out a big sigh. He knew he had to go but he was worried. "Dad, we won't have anything in common."

"You won't know until you meet him. Now get ready to go."

"Well hi," Mrs. Rahn said as she opened the back door of her house. "Come on in."

"Hi, Mrs. Rahn," the boy said as he took off his hat and coat. The house smelled of fresh baked bread, roast beef, and cookies.

"Come in and meet Melvin," she said as she showed the boy to the living room.

Melvin was sitting on the couch, and his face told the story of his journey. He looked scared to death.

"This is Melvin," she said as she made the introductions and tried to get a conversation going.

"Hello," Melvin said.

"Hi."

"Would you boys like some chocolate chip cookies?"

"Sure," came the response from the local."

"Yes Mam," from the traveler.

As she left the living room for the kitchen, they knew they were on their own for conversation that would break the ice and maybe and lead everyone to a point where friendship could have a chance to grow. But, what subject?

Certainly the oyster truck trip would get them talking. Meeting the sheriff for the first time would also work. Talking about his home in Alabama could put him at ease. So would differences in the weather—it was bitterly cold in Nebraska and he knew Alabama was located along the warm Gulf coast. He had yet to see a big body of water like the Gulf. That would be interesting, too.

"Have you seen any rats in the jail?"

"No," came the barely audible response.

"Are there any crooks in the cells next to you?"

"No."

"Do they really only give you bread and water to eat?"

"No."

He looked down at the floor in failure. This guy obviously didn't want to be friends. He was just too different, he thought. All he said was "no." There was just no way to break through the deafening silence. He had done his best and now he just wanted to get away and go home.

"Do ya'all play sports up here?"

He looked up from the floor at the shy voice that was finally asking him a question.

"Sure we do," he said with a smile that was soon answered in kind. "During the winter there's basketball but I'm not very good at that. I'm better at football and we have a great golf course. We also go fishing a lot and the older guys hunt for pheasants in the fall."

"I like to play basketball and fish."

"Where do you fish?"

"Oh we fish from the docks some."

"On the Gulf of Mexico?"

"Ya, on Mobile Bay."

"That must be great. I would love to see the Gulf of Mexico and all of those big ships. Do you have a lot of big ships in Mobile?"

"Some," he said quietly. "What kind of fishin do ya'all do around here?"

"Oh we go fishing for bullheads and suckers in Bow Creek when it's deep enough and once in a while, Mr. Rahn takes us out on his boat on Lewis and Clark Lake. They say the catfish down by the front of Gavins Point Dam are as big as a man."

"That's some big fish."

"How are you boys getting along?" a booming voice said from the back of the house as the back door closed with a bang. Mr. Rahn was home and under his arm was a package from the Globe clothing store. He had been shopping for his young guest. The look of the South would soon be replaced with the look of the West as he started pulling jeans and western shirts from the package and distributing them to the smiling stow-a-way sitting on his living room couch.

"I hope these fit OK" he said as put a small stack of new clothes in the boy's lap. "I thought you might like to go to the basketball game tomorrow night and might need some new things to handle the cold up here."

"Thank you, sir," he said as looked at the new clothes.

"Do you like basketball?"

"Yes sir."

"OK, we'll go. Why don't you come along with us? I'll ask your Dad if it will be OK."

"That would be great, Mr. Rahn."

"I'll run you home so Blanch can get dinner on the table. Have you had dinner?"

"Yup, fried chicken and mashed potatoes and apple pie."

"Well you're welcome to stay and eat some roast beef with us."

"Thanks Mr. Rahn, but I have some homework to do."

"See ya'all tomorrow?" Melvin said as he stuck out his hand for a good-bye shake.

"See ya tomorrow," he said as he gave a much firmer handshake.

"Did you have a good time?" his mother asked as they came through the back door of the family home, escorted by Mr. Rahn.

"Ya."

"What is he like?" she continued. "Is he nice?"

"Ya."

"What did you talk about?"

"Just stuff."

"We're all going to the basketball game tomorrow night if that's OK with you?" Mr. Rahn said in his loud booming voice. He was smiling and enjoying his role as dad for a day. "Blanch is cooking up a storm so don't worry about anything."

"That will be fine." She knew the young stranger and her son were in the care of good hands. The Rahn's were good, hard working people but they couldn't have children. He loved sports and the outdoors and often included this boy in his outdoor activities.

"Yes, Jennifer," the teacher said the next morning at the beginning of the social studies class.

"Did you hear about the boy in jail?"

"Yes," I understand he ran away from home and rode up here in a truck of some kind. That must be quite an adventure."

"Oyster shell truck."

"What did you say?" the teacher asked.

"He rode up here in an oyster truck. His name is Melvin."

"How do you know that?"

"I met him last night. We are going to the basketball game tonight."

From that point on, the rest of his day was filled with questions. What was the boy like? Was he a criminal? Was bread and water all he really had to eat? Was he nice? Was his skin really black?

Around mid afternoon, it started to snow. Big flakes fell from a dark gray sky, which was a sure sign the snow would be deep by nightfall. He hurried home and finished his homework early, and cleared the walks so he would be ready when Mr. Rahn came. Shortly after dinner, a truck parked on the street outside of the house. He already had his coat on and headed out into the snowy night.

"Hi," he said as the door of the truck opened to him. He was squinting as the big flakes hit him in the face, causing him to blink when they hit his eyes.

The windshield wipers slammed down against the building snow at the bottom of the windshield. He could hear the sound of the defrost heat going full speed.

"Pretty good snow going isn't it?" Mr. Rahn said as he stuck out his arm and pulled the boy into the truck. Melvin was sitting in the middle, bundled up from head to toe.

"Hi," he said to his new friend as he slammed the door of the truck. "Pretty cold, huh."

"Yeh, and the snow is building up pretty fast."

"You have to scoop all that snow?"

"Sure. Your neighbors could slip and fall if you don't."

"Is it heavy?"

"Not this stuff. It is still pretty fluffy and not too wet. When it is wet, it is heavy."

"Can you make a snowman out of this snow?"

"Sure. But I don't do that anymore. That's for little kids."

"Oh."

The truck bounced along in the ruts created from other trucks. The city snowplows had not reached that part of town. Since there was a basketball game, they would be clearing the downtown and school areas first and take on the neighborhoods when the snow stopped.

Mr. Rahn parked his truck in a cleared area close to the city auditorium. "We'll boys, button up, here we go."

He opened the door and hopped out of the truck and went around and opened the other door. Melvin was cautious. He gently put his foot down on the shiny, just cleared concrete surface under his foot.

"Is it slippery?" he asked.

"Nope," his friend said. "When it melts and freezes again, it gets really slippery."

"He tested his friend word with his new boots at got out of the truck."

As they headed for the front steps of the auditorium, and the warm glow of the activity inside, Melvin stopped and looked down the street toward the sound of a big engine running fast for a while and then going to idle. He could see a machine mounted on the front of a tractor, with a truck driving slowly alongside. When the big engine ran fast, he could see a stream of white go from the top of the tractor to the back of the dump truck.

"What's that?" he asked Mr. Rahn.

"That's a snow blower. The city maintenance people push the snow into the center of the road using a road grader and then they come along with that snow blower and fill up trucks that take the snow out of town and dump it. By the time the game is over, there won't be any snow on the streets."

"Fast," he said as he watched the snow blower fill the dump trucks.

The basketball gym was packed and every eye in the place was on Melvin. He was having a difficult time balancing Cokes®, popcorn, and candy as the crowd bounced up and down with the pace of the game.

"I can make a jump shot from way out there," Melvin said.

"I ain't any good at basketball. But I can play football and golf pretty good."

"I ain't never played golf. That's a white persons game."

"Black people don't play golf?"

"They can't play on most courses in the South. It ain't allowed. You can caddie some if you have a connection."

"I bet Mr. Rahn will take you golfing if you come back this summer. He's got one of them new gas powered golf carts. It's really fun."

By the half-time buzzer, the boys and Mr. Rahn were once again standing in the concession stand line.

"How about a couple of hot dogs, boys? Give us three hot dogs and three Cokes®," he said to the high school pep club member doing her duty at the concession stand.

As they waited for the second half, other local boys came up to their familiar local friend. They too, were wondering about the stranger. They heard the story of the great adventure. They had never met a black person. They wondered.

Melvin was still shy but he was starting to feel a little more comfortable with the people in this small town. His sad look had been replaced by a smile and his handshake was a little more firm. He was starting to trust his new friend.

When the game ended, the local fans poured out into the cold Nebraska night. Melvin was suddenly hit with a snowball.

"Ouch," he said as he looked at what hit him. "That was hard as a baseball."

"Let's hurry along, Mr. Rahn said as he looked around to see who might have thrown the snowball. "We'll have some hot chocolate and cookies at home."

"Can we go outside for a little while?" Melvin asked.

"Sure," but stay close to the house. "It won't take long for the hot chocolate to be ready," Mr. Rahn said.

The boys got out of the truck and stood in the driveway and watched the snow fall. It was starting to get lighter, a sign that the storm was coming to an end. Melvin leaned down on one knee and pushed his index finger down through the four inches of snow. He looked at the hole his finger made and thought about the feeling.

"Wanna make a snow angel?"

"What's a snow angel?" Melvin asked.

"Here," his friend said. "Just watch."

He lay down in the snow and moved his arms and legs back and forth and got up. "See, he said as he pointed to the pattern in the snow, it looks like an angel."

Melvin looked at the design and smiled. He dropped into another fresh area of snow and did the same thing. He stood up and looked and laughed at his snow angel.

"Is there black snow?" he asked.

"Black snow?"

"Ya, is there black snow?"

"Only when it gets dirty."

"That's dirty white snow. I want to know if there is black snow."

"Not that I know of. Plus it wouldn't look right."

"Why wouldn't it look right?"

"You couldn't see it very well."

"Why couldn't you see it?"

"Look at that pine tree across the street," his friend said.

"See how the white snow sits on the branches? You can see the white snow against the sky. You couldn't see black snow."

"Yes you could," Melvin said. "You could see it if you looked with that white house was behind it."

"Well?" Melvin asked as his friend stood and looked at the tree and the house.

"I'm thinking," he said. "It wouldn't look right."

"If that is all you had ever seen it would look right, wouldn't it?

"Well?"

"I'm thinking."

Melvin picked up a handful of snow, packed it into s snowball and lightly tossed the snowball at his friend, hitting him in the back.

"You asked for it," he said as he tackled Melvin and rubbed a handful of snow in his face. They wrestled and laughed as the rolled around in the snow until Mr. Rahn called them in for hot chocolate and cookies.

"Wanna do something tomorrow?"

"Sure," Melvin said.

"Maybe we could go ice skating if the ice is good."

"Ice skating'?"

"I'll call you tomorrow," his friend said as he got in the truck with Mr. Rahn.

"Looks like you guys are getting along fine," Mr. Rahn said.

"Ya, he's OK We might do something tomorrow if it's OK"

"Sure, that would be fine."

It was almost noon on Saturday when he made the call. "Hi Mrs. Rahn, is Melvin there?"

"Oh, he went home this morning," she said. "The sheriff found his parents and he is on his way back to Alabama. He told me to say good-bye to you."

"I liked him, Mrs. Rahn," he said through the phone. "Thank you for asking me to meet him."

"He was a nice boy, wasn't he," she said. "Maybe we'll see him again some day."

The day never came. Melvin never returned to Hartington but one Hartington boy always wondered about his new friend. Maybe someday a tall black man, with short cut graying hair, will meet a white man who has lost most of his hair, on the streets of some city. Maybe they'll stop for a second, smile, and talk about something in common.

"Excuse me, but is there such a thing as black snow?"

The Music
of Miss Stone

◆

"Twinkle, twinkle little star," his dad said as he looked up from the sports section as his smiling wife.

"You should encourage him," she said as she watched him snap the paper and try to renew his sports concentration. "He can also play Little Brown Jug."

"What do you call that thing?" he asked as he listened to the muffled sound coming from an upstairs bedroom.

"It's called a tonette. They learn to play music and read notes using a tonette and then they'll move on to real instruments."

"Sounds like a hoot owl with gas. Does he know any Sousa marches?"

"Not yet," she said with a twinkle in her eye, "but give Miss Stone a little time and you will really be surprised, you really will be."

Miss Stone came to Hartington with an almost impossible task. Her mission was to bring a new type of music to the town. Hartington High was going to have a high school band and Miss Stone was going to draft kids in grade school in order to do it

"I need to talk to you," Miss Stone said as she caught up with the principal as he walked down the hall toward his office. "We need more space for the band."

"Can't you use the auditorium?"

"The auditorium downtown?" she asked.

"Sure," he answered. "It's only a couple of blocks away."

"Would you like to transport a sousaphone or a bass drum two blocks at seven in the morning and then get that stuff back here in time for the morning bell?" she asked. "How about the coal bin in the grade school? We can clean it up and it's big enough."

"You want to put your band in that old coal bin?"

"I don't see any other room that's big enough, do you?"

"No," the principal answered, "I suppose not."

"Then we can have the coal bin and a small budget to put in some sound absorption and paint?"

"How big of a budget?"

"Small," she answered. "But just think of the return."

"OK, do it," he said as he opened the door to his office and started in. "But keep things under control, OK?"

The old grade school building had been converted to gas heat and there was no longer any need for a giant room with a twenty-foot ceiling that was used to store coal for the old coal-burning furnace.

"What do you think?" she asked the janitor as the two of them peered through the door into the abandoned coal storage room. "Can you clean it up and make it work?"

"That's a pretty tall order," the janitor answered. "We'll have to clean it out and wash it down and then apply a few coats of paint."

"I'll help," she answered. "Let's get cracking."

The janitor cleaned out the room. He painted the blackened walls with several coats of white paint. The upper walls were covered with special material to stop sound from bouncing from wall to wall.

Almost as soon as the last coat of paint dried, she set up sixty folding chairs and a silver music stand in front of each one of them in a big semi-circle. She stood in front of the semi-circle and looked out at the imaginary faces that would soon be looking at her.

"Not high enough," she said.

She turned and started up the newly painted white wooden stairs to the door leading to the basement level of the grade school. She was searching for her best supporter.

"Can you build me a podium?" she asked the janitor. "I need to be higher so the kids can see me."

"I can build anything," he answered. "Just give me a sketch and I will have it done by morning."

Finally she was ready to bring a band to Hartington. She stood on her new podium and looked out at her coal bin band room. It wasn't big enough. It wasn't perfect. But it would do just fine for Miss Stone.

"This will do just fine," she said to herself. "I will build a band in a coal bin," she said as she giggled. "Bring on the kids."

She drew a lot of attention the instant she came to town. She stood a couple of inches over five feet tall and carried a couple of hundred pounds on her short frame. She had short black hair and wore a pair of black, horned-rimmed glasses that liked to keep her busy by sliding down her nose as she waved her hands through the rigors of teaching music.

She could play every instrument in her band and could switch between them as easily as switching a car from park to reverse. That was quite an accomplishment when you consider that her forte was orchestra. Her first love was the warm singing sounds of the strings. When her teaching day ended and the grading and reports were done, her attention turned to the one instrument that no one at this assignment would ever learn how to play, her prized violin.

Unfortunately, at Hartington High, she would not be teaching gifted children the singing sounds of beautiful strings. Her assignment was to teach country kids how to honk in harmony. The band project electrified most of the people in the town. Who would play what? How long before there would be a concert? What would the new band play at the concert? Would the school buy the kids uniforms?

Finally, the day came when the truck from Tom's Music House showed up at school. Miss Stone had a good idea who would play what as she assessed lip structure, kid size, temperament, and personal interest. A trombone for John Miller. A coronet for his younger brother, Kenny. A baritone for Jimmy Buchanan. Another trombone for Bill O'Meara. Bill's mother had to modify the slide with a string so he could tie the string to his finger, and then to the slide. Then short-armed Bill could throw the slide out beyond his reach and hit 7th. position. Mrs. O'Meara measured carefully. If the string was too short, the note would be a little higher than planned—a little sharp. If the string was too long, the note would be a little lower—a touch flat. Either way, Miss Stone's tender ears would know. As Bill grew in size and arm length, his mother was in a constant state of string adjustment. Finally young Bill had grown enough that the string was no loner necessary. He could reach 7th. position on his own—a sure sign of the passage from boy to man.

Pat Powers and Chuck Carkoski got the long black clarinet with all of the shiny silver finger holes. Ann Palmer got a flute—the long tube of chrome that could convert the air of a whisper into the restful sound of morning. And Jamie Wier got the biggest of all, the Sousaphone. It suited his big size perfectly and when he had it in place, it looked like he had been born in this giant horn which surrounded him and turned into a big golden bell right over his head.

Playing all of those horns was only one of Miss Stone's amazing talents. She was also very impressive when she stood in front of her blackboard with the permanently inscribed music staff bars. She stood in front of the blackboard, put the chalk in her left hand, and started writing to the center. Treble clef. Four-four time. One sharp. Eighth note. Eighth note. Quarter note. Pause. When she reached the center of the board, she switched hands and continued to write with her right hand until she reached the other side of the board. None of her attentive students could tell the difference in writing style from one side of the blackboard to the other. And every note, every sharp, every pause, was clearly hummed as she worked along.

It wasn't long before what looked like a band was gathered in what was once a coal bin. She raised her arms above the heads of her young students, most of whom had gone through a little preparation in the smaller music room, and gently guided her small white baton through the coal bin air. As she gently cut through the air with the confidence of a great conductor, the magic mix of brass and woodwinds and drums changed the sounds of Hartington forever. Thank God for spit valves.

Parents have one of the most difficult tasks when faced with having their wonderful children become part of a newly formed band. They endured the awful sounds coming from an instrument and at the same time must encourage the kid to practice.

"Have you practiced today?" she asked her son as he settled in for a night of television watching. It was more than homework that made her ask the question. Her word was on the line because she had to sign a weekly practice slip attesting to the fact that her boys practiced their required three hours for the week.

"I am not going to sign any practice slips if you don't practice," she said. "Now get cracking."

"Honk honk. Honk honk. Honk honk honk. Honk honk. Honk honk. Honk honk. Honk."

"What was that other thing he was playing?" her husband asked.

"The tonette?" his wife asked.

"Yup," he answered. "I think I liked that one better than this coronet. Why is it called a coronet anyway? Isn't it a trumpet?" he asked as he looked up from the paper and focused his attention on the sounds coming from the upstairs bedroom.

"It's a different type of instrument," she answered. "It's fatter than a trumpet and has a different sound."

"Well I guess that is an understatement," he said as he listened to his son miss another note.

Finally, the young band and the patient community were ready for the first public concert. The stage at the city auditorium was too small to hold the sixty-piece band so the band and the audience had to share the basketball court.

The band was dressed in their concert best—black slacks and skirts, white shirts and blouses. Soon the local concert hall started to fill. There were plenty of proud parents, proud relatives, and a large contingent of the local widows club with the variety of white and blue hair.

The band was sitting in several half circle rows with heavy brass in the middle, woodwinds on the left and the cornets and trombones on the right and drums and sousaphones in back. The sounds of the gathering crowd stilled.

Miss Stone appeared from the back stage door, complete with black dress, and corsage. The crowd broke into a big applause. She was a short, heavy woman so she moved her shoulders and arms from side to side with each step. She arrived at the podium somewhat winded, but her smile lit up the audience. She stepped up on the small podium and gave a short bow and extended her right arm with a graceful wave to present her new band. The audience responded with smiles and more applause. Then she turned to her coal bin band. She smiled and she gave them a wink from her twinkling eye and whispered, "show 'em your stuff."

"Honk honk. Honk honk. Honk honk boom. Wha-wha. Wha-wha. Wha-wha. Trill."

"See," the coronet player's mom whispered as she elbowed her husband in the ribs, "I told you they would be good."

The young band was a big hit. So was their beloved teacher.

"I hate our school colors," grumbled one of the band member boys. "Purple and white," he said. In his mind, he pictured purple pants with a white stripe.

"Can you imagine purple jackets with a white "HHS" on the front," he said as he sat with some of his band member friends at an after school cherry Coke® and potato chip gathering at the Cedar Cafe.

"They'll probably have to get an entire flock of purple chickens to surrender their feathers just to make little plumes for the top of our hats."

"As a matter of fact, the uniforms will be gray and have some purple trim, shaker hats with a white plume, and a double set of button going down the front."

The kids turned to see Miss Stone standing behind them. She was a regular at the Cedar Café. She didn't cook and the blue plate special was an important part of her blue note day.

"The sample uniform will be here tomorrow and we'll start measuring everyone for uniforms," she said.

"Are they neat Miss Stone?"

"You can tell me tomorrow night," she said as she smiled and sat down in a nearby booth.

Since band was classified as an activity, practice was not held during regular school hours. Band members had to be in the coal bin at 7:15 in the morning.

"Everyone outside," Miss Stone ordered the sleepy-eyed band members. "It's showtime. We are going to learn how to march."

"I can't do this," complained a cornet player. "If I do that high step stuff like she wants, my mouth piece slips off of my lip. How can you play and still do this other stuff?"

The band roamed at will, through every part of town at the crack of dawn, pounding the drums and blurting out the familiar sound of Sousa marches.

"Must be about 7:30, I can hear the band," became the familiar words from sleepy residents in the morning hours.

"When are you going to march by my home?" interested neighbors often asked their neighborhood musician.

"You'll have to talk to the guy in front who has that funny looking long pole," came the response. "He's the driver."

The sound of a confused foot shuffle was soon replaced with the sounds of crisp deliberate steps like the sounds of a marching army, and the hit and miss of a drum turned into a rumbling rhythm. The old folks who used to peek out of their doors were now out on their porches, in their robes, doing an elderly toe tap to the very recognizable sound of John Philip Sousa.

Eventually, the band marched through all of the neighborhoods in town and right down the middle of Main Street. The entire rush hour of twenty-four cars came to a complete stop, as the local cop ordered cars to stop as the band marched through the four major intersections.

The band was ready and the kids were satisfied they were hot stuff. Miss Stone had trotted along every step of the way reminding the marching musicians to stay in straight lines, mark cadence, and hold the horns high. All the band needed was an invitation to go somewhere and show their stuff.

"Maxine," the principal asked. "Is your band ready to accept this?"

He handed her a letter from the University of Nebraska in Lincoln inviting the band to perform in the band day parade and half-time ceremony at the Nebraska-Missouri football game.

"Charter a bus!" she said as she kissed the invitation and held it up to the sky.

The band kids were wildly excited on the three-hour bus ride to Lincoln. When they arrived at the parade staging area, most of the kids went into small town band shock.

"God," exclaimed one of the shocked band members. "Look at all of these big bands."

They watched as school busses unloaded bands five times as big—complete with twirlers and flag girls. They listened as the big city kids tuned up and started playing tougher music and they deliver it with power, tits, and glitter. The young band was suffering from depression and stage fright.

Miss Stone knew they were a little scared and gave her famous pep talk and her confident wink and down Lincoln's "O" street they went, with her at a fast proud walk all of the way.

The band went on to play The National Anthem at home football games and perform some small half-time shows. Some of the boys had different uniforms than the rest of the band. These band members were also football players and there wasn't enough time to change.

"Miss Stone, are we going to enter a contest?" one of her students asked as they sat in the coal bin waiting for her to pass out the new stack of music on her podium.

"Well kind of," she said as she handed the stack of music to each side of the semi-circle. "Contest is a short name for Music Contest. It's a competition held at Wayne State College. We are going to play three classical selections and a group of five judges will grade our performance."

"What kind of grades?"

"The categories are superior, excellent, good and good God," she said as the band broke into a laugh. "There will be no good-God ratings from any band of mine."

Bach was in for contest but Miss Stone had a small problem. She needed the sound of a French horn and she summoned one of her cornet players to her office to talk about the problem.

"I would like you to play the French horn for the concert band," she said in her gentle attention-getting way.

In an instant, he went from the crack cornet corps to the dreaded job of playing a glorified coiled up moose call. And, to make matters worse, he would have to play it with his not so perfect left hand. He knew he would have to stick his right hand up the moose call's butt to control the pitch of the sound as it came out the rear facing horn. That wasn't a problem but he knew he would have to manipulate the lever-style valves with his left hand, which was far from perfect. But, if there was one person in the world he couldn't say no to, it was this twinkling eyed teacher sitting in the chair in front of him.

"Miss Stone, I don't know if I can play it with my left hand," he said.

"I know you can do it," she said as she smiled at him. "We'll just have to work a little harder than you ever have, but I know you will be just right for the job."

He couldn't say no to someone who was always there to help him take his next step on the confidence ladder of life.

His first test would come at the local concert. His best friend had often performed as a soloist singer but he had never done a solo. The Bach piece called for a French horn solo. It wasn't a long solo but it had to be perfect.

The local crowd grew in size and music appreciation. The band was now dressed in matching uniforms. They played their best Bach. He played his best solo. And, the wink from the podium and the applause from the audience made it clear he had learned and performed well. The band received a superior at contest.

"Miss Stone," he asked his favorite teacher as she took her violin out of the case and prepared to play. "Are you leaving?"

"Yes," she said. "I have an opportunity to start an orchestra. Orchestra is my favorite you know and it is time for me to move on."

"You are just going to leave us like that?"

"Oh no, I am not going to do that," she said as she put her violin back in the case and put her hands on his shoulders. "I am going to leave you with a love for music and another teacher will come and pull more of it out of you. You have a good heart and your heart is where the angels sing. There will be others who will come along in your life and help you learn how to let your soul sing. Nobody ever leaves your life. Just like you will always be part of mine."

Her French horn player went on to college and a career in business. He joined a church even though he wasn't a member of that religion. He knew this church had a performing brass ensemble, a large choir, and a magnificent pipe organ and they loved to play a few of the master's best works.

He ushered at that church and occasionally, the brass ensemble played a Bach piece with a French horn solo. The sound of that French horn stopped him right in his tracks. He looked down at the floor as the tears welled up in his eyes. Even though he hadn't played an instrument in years, he could follow the notes in his mind and remember his gift, the priceless gift of music from the great heart of Miss Stone.

Working
on Main Street

$\blacklozenge$

"If we say there are twenty pounds of potatoes in the bag, make sure their are at least twenty pounds in the bag," he told the boy on his first day. He handed the boy a stack of brown sacks with the small rope style handles and pointed out the scale and the chest high pallet of 100-pound gunnysacks of potatoes.

"Folks can easily check the weight when they get home and if there is less than twenty pounds, they might think we are cheating them on everything. They may never come back to the store again," he instructed the young teenage boy he had just hired.

Chic Becker wanted something special from his store. Sure, he wanted to make a good living, but he also wanted to offer good value and have employees who knew how to package that value with good, honest customer service. He was a short man, balding, and soft-spoken. He wasn't the slave driver type of boss. He was a nice guy trying to do his best.

"Your job is to make sure we give our customers what we promise—honesty, friendliness, and prompt service," he continued. "If you don't do your job right, we'll lose more than a little business, we'll lose the respect of our customers and that's something no store can survive. And, when the ladies up front call out for you, straighten yourself a little and go up there as soon as you can. Don't make folks wait. Let's take care of people promptly."

People Store was in the middle of all of the Main Street action in Hartington, Nebraska. You could park your car free right in front and you were only a couple of steps from the big front glass door. Chances are, you may have to hold the door for someone coming out, and the carryout boy bringing the groceries, or maybe you would have to hold the door for an elderly lady out for her grocery shopping. The door needed a new coat of green paint and the brass handle could use a good polish but Chic hadn't gotten around to that. Once inside, the smell of the specials hit you instantly. Fresh peaches were in. The spices for the holidays had arrived, too. It took only a couple of steps to feel the friendliness of the old store. The wooden floors creaked but still shined from the oil treatment. The store shined like a clean store was supposed to shine. Two checkout lines were in front of the store.

The phone started ringing off the hook just a few seconds after eight on Saturday mornings. Once Chic unrolled the store's green front awning, folks knew their link to the world of wonderful foods was open for business. Marcia was always the first one to get busy.

"Good morning, People's Store. This is Marcia," she said in her friendly smiling voice. She tucked the phone headset between her chin and her right shoulder and started looking for a small green order pad, which was close to her check stand.

"Oh, hi," she knew who was on the other end of the phone as well as most folk's grocery product preference. "Yes, we sure are. Sure, I'd be happy too." Even though you could only hear one side of the conversation, it was clear what was going on. One of the local lady customers wanted to know if the boys were going to deliver groceries and, if so, could Marcia take her order, gather the items for her, and charge it to her account.

Marcia was honest on all things. "They're a little hard," she might say about the early peaches. "Maybe they'll be better next week. The new plums look good. You would like a couple of them? Fine!" She never recommend anything she would not serve her own family.

Once she finished her conversation, she grabbed a metal grocery cart and raced around the store picking up a can of this, a can of that, a loaf of bread, a couple of the best of the customer specified fruit. She squeezed the Charmin® and sniffed the cantaloupe to make sure both were fresh and ready for duty. After she gathered everything listed on the little green pad, she carefully wrote the exact price next to each item, totaled the bill, put all of the groceries in a sack, folded the top of the sack, and stapled the bill to the fold.

"Delivery order!" Marcia hollered to the back of the store.

Chic looked up from his small desk at his new teenage helper. The young boy licked the palm of his hand and ran it through his hair in order to get momentary control of his young growing mane. He made a quick mirror check to make sure his grocery boy white apron was somewhat presentable. He checked his Converse® tennis shoes to make sure they were tied. Now was not the time to trip over untied shoelaces. Then, with a slow jog around the full carts of groceries and the farm wives carefully scanning the prices and the products, he navigated the aisles to the front of the store like a fast sports car trying to get through rush hour traffic in L.A. Chic smiled as he watched the boy head for the front.

Marcia was swamped ringing up orders for the farm wives who had arrived in town and now filled the aisles of the little store. There were no cash registers with scanning equipment in those days and each order had to be rung up on an old adding machine. After each entry, Marcia pulled the handle on the right side of the old machine in order to print the amount. She carried on a conversation with the customer at the same time. She put up with that hectic Saturday pace and never lost her smile.

"Order up front," she hollered again.

The race was on again. With each juke and move to get through the crammed cart crunch came an always-polite smile and "Good morning. Excuse me." The ladies hardly noticed as the boy skillfully moved through the aisles. They certainly weren't bothered by the temporary distraction caused by the young lad. Most of them knew his family and were interested in seeing what kind of boy he was. He seemed well mannered and polite and each of them would have their turn with him sometime during the day.

"Would you please take Mrs. Morton's groceries to her car?" Marcia asked.

"Sure," he said. "How are you today Mrs. Morton?"

Carry out was just as necessary to the ladies as the charge accounts and delivery. The store parking lot was the same parking lot used by every other Main Street business. You could pick a spot and pull in diagonally. There were no parking meters to fool with. You could stay as long as you like. Late arriving shoppers may have to park some distance away from the store they planned to shop.

"Let's see," the boy thought as he started to hoist two large bags of groceries, "this farm wife drives a brown '57 Chevrolet®. She said it was two blocks down the street. He needed to take these two sacks, the case of Mason® jars (necessary for canning everything from corn to chicken) and twenty pounds of russets potatoes. He knew there was never less than twenty pounds of potatoes per bag because he sacked and weighed them himself and his gentle boss and store owner instructed him to never be short.

"That's a big order," Marcia said. "Can you handle all of that stuff at once?" He strained with the formless sacks, the case of jars, and the twenty pounds of potatoes hanging from two fingers on his right hand as the rest of his hand cradled one of the grocery sacks.

"No problem."

He turned and followed the lady out the front door, being very careful to use his foot to hold the heavy wooden door open for an elderly lady entering the store.

"Oh, thank you," the lady said as she stopped and looked more carefully at the boy. "Why you are Bun's boy, aren't you?"

"Yes Mam." He could feel the groceries shift a little and raised his right knee to push the bottom of one sack so he get better leverage. He needed a better position to help give him control of the sack without smashing the loaf of bread or breaking the dozen fragile eggs that rested comfortably on top of the paper sack. It was packed with canned goods, cake mix boxes, and long stalk of celery that anchored the inside corner of the sack.

"Well tell your mother hello for me," the lady said as she entered the store.

"Yes Mam, I sure will."

The car he needed to find was two blocks "down" the street. The lady whose groceries he carried had decided to go the other way and shop at the clothing store. In those days, the streets did not have any street signs on them. Everything was referred to as either up the street, which was North, or down the street, which was South.

Two blocks down the street would take him by most of the storefronts that lined Main Street. The Cedar Cafe was busy with morning customers having breakfast and their morning coffee. The load was shifting so he gave it another boost with his leg.

"Oh, excuse me!" he said as he bumped into a customer coming out of the Cedar Café. The sack obscured his vision. He couldn't see who he had bumped into.

"Well look who is carrying groceries this morning."

He turned the sack to see who had bumped into and who recognized him.

"Oh hi Miss Stone," he said as he recognized his favorite teacher. She was grinning from ear to ear as she watched him balance the big load of groceries.

"Do you need a little help?" she asked as she made a move to help him stabilize the load.

"No," he said confidently. "I've got it handled."

"You're sure about that?" she said.

"Yup."

"OK, then," she said as she moved out of his way. "Good luck."

The musty smelling Feed and Seed store was the next store. If there was an old brown DeSoto® parked in front, there was a chance he might run into his friend, Old Henry. Hopefully the encounter would have some warning however. Hegert Hardware was on the corner. He was anxious to hear from Mr. Hegert because he was saving his earnings to buy a brand new Remington® 870 pump shotgun from him. Pheasant season was only a few weeks away and he was excited about learning to hunt.

One block down and time to cross the street. Wintz Furniture was on the corner. Tubby Lammer's Office was on the second floor and the VFW Club was in the basement. Wid Burney's Farm Management Company was next. Finally he reached the best business in town, Miller Motor Company and it's exceptionally terrific owner, his dad. He made his one footed load adjustments and slowed down a little bit when he reached the showroom windows of the garage so his dad would have a good opportunity to see his son working himself to death.

In the same building as his dad's Ford® garage was the major competition, Hahn Chevrolet®. It was a handy arrangement for anyone who had come to town and hadn't decided on which brand he wanted to buy. It was only a short walk to compare product and a few more short walks to start a price battle between the two dealers.

The city auditorium was next. He was starting to worry. He was now two blocks "down" the street and no '57 brown Chevrolet® in sight. Maybe the nice farm lady really meant "up" the street?

He stood on the corner with two sacks of groceries, twenty pounds of potatoes hanging on two very strained young fingers, and a case of Mason® jars tucked under an arm which was also trying to cradle another grocery sack without crushing the eggs and bread. The load was extra clumsy and heavy when he realized the car might be four blocks in the other direction. Worst of all, he would have to move quickly by the Miller Motor windows, hope that Old Henry wouldn't spot him, pray that Miss Stone was long gone, and that Marcia was too busy to notice the embarrassed boy, who couldn't follow directions, sneak past the front of the store. He also knew his boss would soon start to wonder where his wandering grocery boy had gone. After all, it shouldn't take that long to go two blocks and deliver two bags of groceries, a case of Mason® jars, and a twenty pound bag of potatoes.

Auditorium. Hahn Chevrolet®. Miller Motor. Farm and Ranch Company. Wintz Furniture. He had reached the corner and so far, so good. His dad was busy on other things. He took a second to look both ways—Ernie Putter could be coming up the side street.

Hegert Hardware. Feed Store. Good deal he thought, Old Henry's car was gone. Miss Stone was gone. Step lively past the People's Store, young lad. He dashed by Tina Perk's Dress Shop, Dr. Lammer's Dentist Office, the Bank of Hartington, and, the Coast to Coast® store. He wondered if the guys waiting in the chair line at the Barber Shop under the bank could see his arms and legs straining from the grocery load as they looked up through the basement level street windows?

This intersection was often a good place to see if he could spot his Uncle Bill. The bank and the Goetz Hardware Store across the street both had tall glass windows with a special window ledge about waist high. His Uncle Bill's often sat on one of those ledges as he sat visiting with one of the Bruning brothers, or tipping his Dekalb® corn seed hat to the farm ladies as they passed by.

"Kind of a heavy load there, young man," he heard a voce say as he passed the bank window ledge. His view was still blocked but he recognized the voice.

"Hi Uncle Bill."

"Need a hand there young man?" his uncle asked.

"Nope. I've got it. Thanks though," he said as he boosted the sack with his knee again.

The sidewalk and streets were busy. Saturday was the day when the area farm families all came to town. It was their chance to stock up on all kinds of needed provisions including the news of the weeks, often exchanged in the store aisles, the window ledges, or on a chance meeting along the street. Kids ran up and down the street until dark, stopping to buy an occasional sack of popcorn from the guy who ran the popcorn machine in front of the Hartington Hotel. Some kids stopped at the Schulte Drug Store and sat at the soda fountain and sipped on a cherry Coke®, or chocolate soda made with fizz water right from an old fashioned fountain. If they had a big allowance, you might see them eating a bag of potato chips or they might take in a movie at the Lyric Theater across the street from the Ford® garage.

Some country boys shared the cost of a ticket with a young city damsel—no hanky-panky though or the theater owner would have that flashlight in your face in a matter of seconds. If the film broke or the camera bulb burned out, you could hear people stomping their feet until he got his movie running again.

The adults who might to cut a little of the farm dust from their throat could stop by either the Chief Bar, or Charlie's Bar for a short nip and a few hands of a card game called sheephead.

It wasn't a good idea to stay long or park in front of the bars, however. Word traveled fast and reputations were at stake. There could be hell to pay if the wife shopping for groceries over-heard the ladies in the next aisle talking about a new drunk who just happened to be her husband.

He was really tired now. His arms and fingers were numb and hurt from the weight. His young muscles bulged as they started to cramp. He was now using his knee to adjust the load every few feet. The bread and eggs were slowly feeling the pressure of his arm as gravity and lack of energy took their tool. He was ready to drop everything.

"Where the hell is that damn car?" he said under his breath.

It had to be just across the street right next to Globe Clothing, he thought. He had no choice but to quicken the pace. The load was moving lower, pulling against what little force he had left. Safely across the street, he hurried past Globe Clothing owned by whistling and always smiling owner. Next was the repair shop owned by Robbie Robbins. Finally, at long last, the brown '57 Chevrolet® parked in the front of Gerry Miller Implement, his father's cousin and friendly neighborhood John Deere® farm equipment dealer.

"Just a few more steps, please God, give me enough strength to go a few more steps." he mumbled as his depleted strength was lost to the force of gravity. He was almost there when the flimsy rope handle on the twenty-pound potato sack broke. The potatoes bounced like malignant tennis balls and started to roll in wild directions out onto Main Street and down the hill.

"Awe dammit," he hollered in agony as he heard that awful squish sound a truck or car makes as the tires roll over the randomly rolling potatoes—twenty pounds, squish, sixteen pounds, squish, fourteen pounds.

"Awe, God, dammit!" he hollered as he tried his best to put the other bags and case of jars on the street next to the car without spilling the other sacks. He desperately grabbed at the fast moving, street free spuds. He crawled under parked cars to get the remaining ones. He raced along the gutter before the storm drain could claim more of them. His white apron was now covered with grease and dirt. His hair was wet with sweat. His arms were so numb that he had to command them to work. He was in a desperate race against tires and time and his ego and honor were at stake. He dashed into the street to catch the remaining free rolling soon-to-be French fries when he heard a sound that caused his heart to stop and his head to snap towards the traffic to his back.

"Honk, Honk, Honk!" came the sound from an old International® pickup bearing down on him. The driver could see him but he knew he wouldn't stop. It was the old German carpenter, Ernie Putter, who could make the pickup go but never took time to learn how to make it stop. He just honked the horn at people and expected people to get out of the way. The boy jumped out of the way as the old carpenter's truck crushed the remaining potatoes.

By now, everyone within ear range was looking at the Kamikaze carpenter's truck and trying to figure out why he was honking in the middle of the block. He usually did not start honking until just a few feet before the stop sign he was planning to run.

Chic soon had the answer to where his new grocery boy had gone.

"Did you hear that old Ernie tried to run down one of your boys and killed a whole twenty pound bag of potatoes?" He watched as the young boy stumbled back into the store, covered with dirt, sweat, and grease.

"We need better potato sacks," the boy said in a defeated voice as he held out the broken sack and the remaining five or so pounds of the farm lady's order. He headed for the back of the store and soon reappeared with another big sack of potatoes that he carried tightly in front of him with both arms. In angered, embarrassed silence, he went out the front door and disappeared up the street.

By ten that night, when everyone had gone home and back to the farm, the city tractor was busy pulling the trailer with the big water tank street washer, up and down Main Street washing all of the Saturday mess away. All that remained from the night before was the embarrassing memories of a fourteen year old boy and a farm lady telling her friends that she got twenty-five pounds of potatoes for the price of twenty at that friendly People's Store in Hartington.

It Looks
a Little Threatening

$\blacklozenge$

The family Scottie stood patiently at the back door of the house waiting for someone to let her out so she could take care of her morning business. The mother was busy ironing a giant stack of family laundry created by a husband and three boys. Her pace quickened as she noticed a change on the television screen. She started ringing her hands as if she was applying hand lotion but chapped hands were not her problem. Her problem was a silent one. It showed up in the spring in the upper right hand corner of the television set. It was just the letter "w." Her middle son walked into the back room and noticed the dog patiently waiting by the door.

"Need to go out Penny?" he asked as the dog bounced on her paws from the attention or the more urgent need to get outside. He went to the door and opened it, pushed the screen door open and dog and boy hopped out into the morning spring air.

He sat down on the step and started to sip orange juice from the blue plastic cup he carried. He watched the dog as she did her business, scratched her paws against the grass and walked slowly across her yard, checking the scent of those critters that dare challenge her territory. Then she turned, sat down on her haunches and started to sniff the sky and scan the horizon off to the southwest. He watched her and wondered what had her attention as she sat almost motionless, except for her slowly moving head. Finally, she turned and ran back to the door.

"Want back in the house, girl?" the boy asked as the dog looked at him.

Normally, she barked when she wanted back in the house, but today, she looked at him and made no sound at all. He opened the door and she scurried into the house.

"You kids stay close to home this afternoon," his mother ordered. "There are storm warnings out for this area."

"Mom," her son said, "we ain't never going to get a tornado here."

Conditions were ripe for the formation of huge, billowing thunderstorms and tornadoes. Tornadoes come in long stringy sizes that dangle like a whip from the nasty billowing black and gray clouds, or they can be a mile wide at the bottom and can ingest an entire small town with a train-sounding gulp.

"And what makes you the weather expert of the family?" she asked.

"There just ain't going to be one today."

"Well when I was a little girl…"

"I know Mom, you tell that story every time it rains."

She had good reasons for her fear. When she was a small farm girl, there were no warnings. No sirens. No radio broadcasts. No slick weatherman cutting into your favorite show with an instant Doppler radar reports. No little "w."

Her first tornado experience came when her father ran across the family farmyard at full speed, snatched her from the ground like a fumbled football, and dove into the damp family cave that served a dual purpose of storm protection and potato storage.

She remembered the roar folks with first hand experience talk about. She remembered an eerie stillness after a few minutes. She remembered her father picking her up and taking her from the dampness of a midday disaster. The house was gone. The barn was gone. The tool shed was gone. Nothing remained but piles of wood, frantic livestock, and a bewildered family.

Every time the little "w" appeared on the television screen, she remembered every detail of her experience. Her family never had the chance to form their own opinion.

She opened the back door and looked toward the southwest. She could see puffy clouds and dark blue sky. She could feel the humidity and the heat. Everything was all set in tornado alley to produce an interesting evening.

By mid afternoon, the small white puffy clouds were growing into towers of angry looking cotton, forming a line across the Nebraska prairie. Trouble was growing. She watched the television for news. Nothing yet. Afternoon heat turned the small storms into big storms. The squall line would soon start to move across the prairie, dumping its variety of hail, rain, and maybe, a tornado.

"We interrupt this program to bring you a special weather announcement from the National Weather Service."

Her head snapped around to see the soap opera disappear and the words "weather warning" centered in the screen as the announcer continued to read the information.

"A tornado warning is in effect for Antelope and Knox Counties until 4:30 this afternoon. Sheriff's deputies confirm a tornado touchdown two miles northwest of Elgin, Nebraska moving Northeast at thirty miles per hour. Persons in the vicinity of Neligh, Norfolk should take cover immediately."

"Get to the basement!" she hollered out the back door. She looked around the back yard. None of her boys were there. They had roamed off to the call of summer. "I told them to stay close to home," she said as she anxiously looked at the billowing clouds to the Southwest.

She ran out to her car and started her search for her boys. One was in the park with his friend Old Henry. "Get home," she hollered through the car window. "There's a tornado coming."

She knew they could get some warning if the tornado actually did make it as far as Hartington. The fire siren would sound with a long blast which one could barely hear through the blasting winds and thunder of the approaching thunderstorm. By then, it might be too late to find shelter in time. She hoped her other two boys heard he earlier warnings, took note of the darkening sky, and headed for home. This was not their first storm experience. After a few Nebraska springs, one could develop a feel for the spring and summer days which had the makings for a good siren blast—muggy morning air, plenty hot, and small puffy clouds in the early hours of the morning.

As she drove down the likely streets where her other two boys might be, she listened to the car radio.

"We interrupt our regular broadcast for this special weather statement from the National Weather Service. A tornado warning is now in effect for the Norfolk area. State Troopers have spotted a tornado on the ground eight miles west of Norfolk moving Northeast at thirty miles per hour. People in the Pierce and Randolph areas should take cover immediately."

"It's coming right at us," she said to herself as she scanned the streets, backyards, and alleys. She spotted another one of her boys at Faulk's station.

"Get home," she said, "there's a tornado coming."

The boy got up from the step in front of the station and looked at the growing clouds in the West and South.

"Get moving, right now," she ordered. Maybe the youngest was home by now, she thought. She turned the corner and headed for home.

She parked the car and ran to the house. The youngest son was watching TV. At the same time, her middle son came through the back door and she could see her oldest son riding up the hill.

She looked for her portable radio and flashlight. "OK you birds, get to the basement."

"Where's Penny?" her middle son asked as he looked around the dark basement. The family pooch would have nothing to do with that damp, cold, and often mouse-infested basement

The boys could tell the wind was increasing as the big pines in the Rossiter yard started to announce the arriving storm.

"The hell with the dog, you stay right where you are and cover your head!" she snapped as she herded her sons to the basement.

"Mom, there is blue sky overhead."

"There is a tornado in Norfolk and Randolph and we'll be next."

"Mom that's an hour away. It will never reach here."

The oldest son headed up the stairs. "You stay put, mister."

"Mom, there is no storm. I ain't gonna stay down there if there ain't no storm."

"There is going to be. I can feel it and the weather people are saying it so you stay put."

"Mom, there isn't any tornado!" he protested as he continued up the steps. "I am going to fix something to eat."

She stepped up on an orange crate and looked through the small window that faced the South. It was still sunny. She could see clouds tops to the distant south but nothing directly overhead. "Well, OK, I'll fix something to eat but nobody leaves the house. Understood?"

"Yes Mom," the boys said in unison as they climbed the steps out of the dingy basement.

As she came out of the basement, she looked at the television. The "w' was still in the corner but local programs played on. She heard a car door slam, which meant her husband, was home from work. She pointed at the TV set when he came through the back door.

"Tornado warnings?" he asked.

"Norfolk and Randolph," she answered.

"Well that's quite a ways away," he said. "It will probably fall apart before it gets here. What's for dinner?"

"Sandwiches," she said. "I was busy rounding up your boys and didn't have time to put the casserole in the oven."

"My boys?" he said as he looked at the three boys digging sandwich meat out of the fridge. "Now they're my boys?"

"I told them to stay close to home because of the weather and they went off all over creation."

"Mom," the oldest said as he pulled the Tupperware® full of lunchmeat out of the bottom shelf of the fridge, "we can't stay around here all day just because the weatherman thinks there might be some kind of storm. He's wrong most of the time anyway."

"We interrupt local programming to bring you this special weather statement. A Tornado watch has been issued for Cedar and Dixon counties until seven this evening. Conditions are favorable for development of tornadoes and thunderstorms with damaging winds and hail. Stay tuned for further details."

"Get to the basement!" she cried out.

"That's a watch, not a warning, Mom."

"Just relax dear," her husband said. "They'll let us know in plenty of time."

He and his middle son headed for the big wooden porch, which surrounded most of the house. They sat down on an old porch swing and started to eat their sandwiches and watch the clouds overhead.

"It's getting pretty dark, Dad."

"Nothing to worry about yet," the father said as he scanned the heavens. The sun is just starting to set. That's why it is getting dark so early. When the sun gets below the cloud layer, it will lighten up a bit."

A few drops of rain started to thump against the porch roof as the wind picked up. In the distance they could hear thunder.

"One two three four five six…" the boy counted as he could see lightning off in the distance. "Six miles away, Dad."

The rain picked up to a light steady pour. The thunder rumbled and shook the house.

"If you get a heavy rain first, you don't have to worry about tornadoes," the boy's dad said as the boy continued to count the seconds from lightning flash to sound.

"It's getting closer, Dad. Are we going to have a tornado?"

"It gets dead still right before a tornado comes," he said as they watched the rain pour from the overflowing porch roof gutter.

Off in the distance, he could hear a faint rumbling sound. It sounded like a freight train.

"Dad, is that a tornado?" he asked as he could see his dad's attention now focused on the rumbling sound, too.

"I don't think so." His dad still seemed very unconcerned as he watched the heavy rain obscure the neighbor's house. The rain fell in sheets. His mom had not made a peep. The rumble seemed to be getting a little louder. The wind was also picking up a bit.

Suddenly his dad jumped to his feet as he watched two trees from the Dywer's yard fall across the highway. At the same time a section of grain bin dropped right in front of them.

"Maybe we should go to the basement," his dad suggested.

He watched as his father's eyes darted from ground to sky as the debris started to fall throughout the neighborhood. The fire siren sounded about the same time his mother did. The real thing was less than a block away bouncing around the town like it was on a rezoning mission. The family raced for the basement.

"Hurry!" his mother screamed as she followed her sons down the basement steps. "Oh God, hurry!" The power went out and the basement went dark except from the flashes of lightning which were non-stop. Thunder rattled the windows and the canned goods on the dark shelf.

"Where is the flashlight," the father asked. A light pierced the darkness as she turned on the flashlight and the radio. She turned the tuning knob through a variety of sharp static discharged from the lightning.

"Folks in the Hartington area should take cover immediately," they could hear through the static, "Sheriff's deputies have sited a tornado two miles west of Hartington heading Northeast." The wind sucked and pulled against the windowpane. It roared like a giant angry beast overhead.

"That's an understatement," the oldest son said. "It's probably already gone by now."

"You stay put," his mother ordered as she pointed her finger at him.

The father got up from his folding chair and started up the steps. "I am going to have a look and see what's going on."

"No!" she hollered out. She remembered the wind pulling against the storm cellar door and in one final grab, pulling it from its hinges. She remembered seeing the edge of the black plume, almost directly above, spinning full of black dirt and debris, and daring them to come out and try to stand against its power.

"You guys stay put," the father said as he went up the stairs. He would take the dare. He was the mayor of this small town and he needed to see what was left of it.

She could barely hear his footsteps as he walked across the kitchen floor above them. The thunder still rocked the house and the flashes of lightning turned early night into bright daylight. She heard the back door open and heard him run down the sidewalk to the car.

"Mom, I am going upstairs, too." The oldest son said as he stood up and started toward the steps.

'Stay put."

"But Mom, Dad went. It's got to be gone by now."

"You stay put. There could be another one."

An hour passed as the driving rains turned to a gentle sprinkle. The thunder diminished as the squall line moved out of the area. The middle son got up on the orange crate and looked out the small windows.

"It's over, Mom," the oldest son said as he headed for the stairs.

Through the night air, they could hear the warning siren start blowing again. "You are not going anywhere," she said. "I wish he hadn't gone. Oh God, here comes another one."

"Mom," he said, "I can see stars. Go upstairs and call the operator."

In the days before dial telephones, you picked up the phone and the friendly operator connected you with anyone. The operator also knew everything there was to know in a small town. She knew who talked to whom. Some say she knew what they talked about. But on this night, the operator knew why the siren was sounding. She was the one who flipped the switch.

"OK, I'll call, but none of you move, understand?" She started up the stairs, still ringing her hands as she slowly climbed each step. She had done this slow walk before. Every noise and smell came back to her. All she could hear through the stillness was the last of the rain running over the gutter and onto the sidewalk below.

"Francis," she said through the phone headset, "are the tornadoes gone? Oh, then what was that last siren? Oh. We'll thank you Francis."

She hung up the phone and headed to the basement door. "Boys, she called out through the basement door, "You can come up. That was a fire call. The Fleming's barn is on fire."

"See Mom," the oldest son said as they all came through the basement door at the same time, "we sat down there for nothing. What a bunch of fradiecats."

"That could have been a tornado, you know. I just did not hear the fire truck leave town. Anyway, it's good practice to do this," she said.

It wasn't long before stillness returned and the western sky started to clear. The tornado had done its damage and was now moving through the countryside Northeast of town. The siren pierced the eerie stillness with the up and down rhythm of the all clear.

The family soon learned the three prize trees in front of the old high school had been topped at the ten foot level. The roof of the food market had been lifted and moved a foot or so. A small car had been picked up out of a used car lot and was now sitting in the front window of the Feed and Chick store across the street. A couple of small sheds down by the railroad tracks had been destroyed. By tornado standards, this one was a whimp—probably one of those long whip ones which danced around town playing a game of powerful Pac-Man®. No lives were lost. A few trees had been reshaped. A few flimsy sheds had been destroyed.

Only one member of the family had correctly interpreted all of the signs of the approaching tornado and sought shelter in the basement.

"What's that scratching noise?" the mother asked.

The boy opened the basement door and the family Scottie dashed out. From then on, the boy watched the dog very carefully when a thunderstorm dropped by for a visit. When his trusty dog pointed her nose to the southwest, perked up her ears, and stopped everything she was doing, so did the boy. In his mind, no warning was ever better.

In Search
of a Little Sin

◆

"Well are you going to do it or not?" his friend asked him as they drove slowly down 2nd Street in Yankton, South Dakota.

"That place doesn't look right," he said as he worried about the danger of getting caught. The last thing in the world he wanted was to see was his dad in the waiting room of the Yankton police station as they processed him for trying to buy beer when he wasn't old enough to buy beer.

"What about that dance hall north of Yankton?"

"Ya, we'll go out there," he said. He heard that this little dance hall would sell beer to anyone.

The dance hall was a renovated small country church. The dance hall was in the main part of the old church and the bar was in the basement.

"You stay here," he said as he got out of the car. "If you get antsy, the guy might get wise and start checking ID."

He was seventeen and looked older than his buddy so he was nominated to make the buy. They were after a case of "panther piss"—3.2% beer. Regular beer had a higher alcohol content so 3.2% was a low octane fuel for high-energy eighteen-year-old kids. Nebraska law didn't allow 3.2% beer or buyers or consumers under the age of twenty-one.

There were only a few cars in the converted church parking lot and it was very dark. A lone light hung from a single pole protecting the privacy of all those who came. He started to worry even more. No dance at the church. No crowd at the church. No people at the church. The bartender would have plenty of time to make his decision. That could be bad news for the borderline looking boy. He knew it was now or never. He had to choose between being the buyer and getting the prestige or being the chicken and getting the scorn.

He stopped for a minute in front of the door to gather his courage. He looked back at his buddy waiting in the car, peering through the window like a pup waiting for the master to return. He cleared his throat and focused on dropping his voice an octave or two. He wrinkled his forehead to put on his best older guy face. He felt ready as he pushed the bar door open.

Four older men sat at the bar and the bartender leaned on the bar visiting with the man closest to the waitress stand. He went up to the stand and waited for service.

"Evenin," the boy said as he rested one arm on the bar and looked the bartender right in the eye.

"Can I help ya son?" the bartender asked as his eyes pierced right through boy's head. This guy looked like the type that would want to see three forms of ID.

"Gimmie a case of 3.2 Bud® cans," he said in his best John Wayne voice.

"I assume you are old enough," the bartender asked as he looked the boy right in the eyes and waited to see if young John Wayne would blink.

"Hell ya," he said as he pulled his wallet out of his jeans and slapped it down on the bar as if he was ready to prove his age.

The bartender looked at him for a couple of very long seconds and then he grinned as he turned and walked to the beer cooler. He soon returned with a the case of beer

"You did say Bud®, didn't you son?" The bartender chomped on the toothpick as the boy handed him a twenty-dollar bill.

As the bartender turned around to the cash register and rang up the sale, the boy looked at the man sitting at the bar next to waitress stand. The man was wearing a dark brown jacket and the boy noticed the patch on the man's shoulder as he picked up his case of beer and turned for the door. The patch said deputy sheriff. The man turned and looked at him and smiled.

"Bet you're glad I'm off duty, ain't ya?"

"See ya, thanks," the boy said as he ignored the deputy and went out the door like a shot out of a gun. Once he cleared the door, he stopped for a second to let his shakes subside.

"That wasn't shit," he said as he opened the car door and handed the case of beer to his buddy. He started the car and sped off into the night, a hero in his friend's eyes and a new story soon be told at the Skylon Ballroom.

They had a thirty-mile drive ahead of them since they had elected to make the buy at the old converted church. The drive called for his best behavior. He worried the deputy might call in and let his on-duty friends know young John Wayne was headed for Yankton.

"Yahoo!" his friend hollered out as he popped open the first two beers. The beer sprayed all over the car.

"Come on! Geeesss. What if we get stopped?" he said. "The car smells like a brewery. God, if my dad smells this, I will be grounded until I am thirty. Take it easy, OK?"

He drove the speed limit and not a mile over it as he entered the Yankton city limits. On the turn past the hospital, he spotted a Yankton city police car, waiting patiently for a speeder to come down the highway from Charlie's Pizza House. The cop looked at his 1959 red and white two door Ford® as they went by. Normally, on a hill like this, he would shift the column shift to second gear so the glass pack mufflers could shatter the night quiet but this was no time to attract attention.

He looked in the rear view mirror, cautious to not make it obvious that he was looking. At the same time, his friend turned and looked back at the cop

"Damn, he's coming!"

Sure enough, the headlights of the cruiser came on as the cop pulled out into traffic, only one hundred feet behind.

"I am doing the speed limit," he said as he started to get nervous. "Get those beers under the seat and put a jacket or something over the rest of it."

His friends jumped into action. "No," he hollered out, "don't be obvious about it. He'll stop us for sure."

The cruiser maintained his distance but kept the same speed. He hoped his speedometer was accurate. He wondered if his tail and brake lights were working. He prayed that the dealer license plate, attached to the bumper with spring clamps, had not fallen off on the way to and from the church.

"Two more blocks and we can turn toward the bridge," his buddy said. He turned the right turn signal on. "Not yet!" his friend said. "Wait another block."

He looked in the rear view mirror. The cruiser's turn signal came on.

"I have to turn. His turn signal just came on. Don't look!" he said as his friend started to turn around and look, "he'll stop us for sure."

He turned a block early. The cruiser followed. He put his turn signal on again to make up for the wrong turn and get him on course for the approach to the bridge over the Missouri River and back to the safety of Nebraska. The cruiser followed.

"Why doesn't he stop us?" his buddy asked. "He doesn't have a good reason to stop us, does he?"

"Just be cool," he told his friend. "We only have a block to go."

He made the last turn and the big bridge that crossed the Missouri River was right in front of them. The cruiser turned, too.

"He can't follow us into Nebraska, can he?" his buddy asked. "Maybe he is radioing ahead to the Nebraska State Police or the sheriff."

"Just stay cool. Look normal."

They crossed the bridge into Nebraska and at the first intersection, the cruiser turned around and went back to South Dakota.

"Yippee! We did it," cheered his buddy as more tap tops broke the tension and more beer sprayed around the car.

"OK, now watch for radar traps," he told his friend. "They say one of the troopers runs with his lights off and gets right behind you and turns everything on at once."

"I'd shit if that happened to me," his friend said.

"Well they like to hide in those country road cuts that obscure the view of their car until you are right on them."

"Who's playing at the dance tonight?" he asked his buddy.

"Six Fat Dutchmen."

"I can't dance to that stuff."

"You can't dance."

"I can too."

"When was the last time you danced? I ain't never seen you on the dance floor. You are too shy."

"I ain't shy."

"When was the last time you were out on a date?"

"Friday."

"With who?" his buddy asked.

"There were lots of us. At the beach party at Gavins Point."

"That ain't a date," his friend chided him. "A date is one on one."

"Well, then it has been a while."

"Look out!" his friend hollered as the light picked up two red dots out in the dark ahead of them. He swerved just in time to miss a mule deer looking straight at them. "Damn they're dumb."

"I spilled beer all over my shirt. God dammit. My dad is going to kill me."

They could see the lights of Hartington in front of them as they crossed the last big hill from north of town. There was a steady steam of lights off in the distance, a clear signal that folks were already heading for the dance or taking their turn driving up and down Main Street and out to the dance hall to see who was around.

They bypassed the downtown parade and headed straight for the dance hall parking lot. He parked the in the back row, away from the lights and the prying eye of the local cop if the officer decided to cruise through the lot looking for underage drinkers.

"What's this stuff?" he asked as one of red-haired female friends handed a bottle through the driver's side window.

"Slow Gin," she said with a twinkle in her eye. "Mix it with a little 7-Up® and it's great."

You could hear the sounds of the Six Fat Dutchmen all over town. The Quonset style ballroom had big screened window openings to allow the cigarette and cigar smoke and loud blasts of the tuba player join the breeze and linger over the town below.

The usual crowd of a couple of hundred people danced around the big wooden floor as the polka band played away. Most folks planned to pace both their drinking and dancing so they could make it through the night or at least through the Dutchmen's rendition of the "The Flying Dutchman," a polka that could turn the dance floor into hurling bodies.

"You going in?" she asked as she poured some more slow gin into his empty cup.

"Not yet," he said as he watched her pour the booze and look around to make sure nobody was watching, cop or friend of her parents.

His buddy stuffed two can of beer in his letter jacket and opened the door. "I'll catch up with you later," he said as he bounded off into the night.

"Got any more mix?" he asked.

"Just this," she said as she poured a thimble full of 7-Up® on top of the half glass of slow gin. "Kill it."

He looked at the glass, bobbed his head in her direction, and grinned. The gin and the beer were taking hold.

"Okie Dokie," he said as he tipped the glass up and gulped and chewed his way through the liquid. The overflow ran down the side of his mouth and down his neck and put the traces on his shirt collar.

"You trying to get me drunk, ain't ya?" he said as he rested his chin on the car door.

"Let's go in and get a Sloppy Joe and some coffee," she said as his strong young body suddenly turned into spaghetti.

"Okie, dokie," he said as he stepped away from the car, tripped and fell forward into a water puddle. "Dammit," he said as he got up, "I hope to hell that wasn't a piss puddle."

In this part of the parking lot, relief was only an open car door away but most guys with class at least went behind the cars. The back row at the dance hall was not the place to be, especially if you were a teenager, a drunken teenager, and if any of your parent's friends were at the dance. In fact, the back row was the worst place to be if any of your parent's enemies were at the dance. Friends might take a parent aside but enemies started rumors and those rumors created reputations.

"Can you walk?" she asked him as she helped him up and brushed some of the dirt off of his pants.

"Hell ya," he said as he teetered to regain his five foot eleven inch standing. He bobbed from left to right for a few seconds and then seemed to center. "Maybe you better let me lean on you a little," he said as he put his arm around her shoulders and started to kiss her neck.

"OK, she said as she started toward the hall, "but you'll have to straighten up when we get to the door. "He won't let you in if you look drunk."

"He'll let me in."

The owner was the gruff man who could throw drunks out just as easy as he could throw a bale of hay up on a hay wagon. He was well liked in his community. Most folks thought of him as a fair and honest man and that was as nice a reputation as one could have in a small town.

He knew the boy. He knew the girl. He watched most of the kids in this town and the countryside go from choir boys and alter boys to teenage boys trying to look like they were still drinking chocolate milk and just having a temporary balance problem.

"Hi," the boy said as he did his best to walk by like normal.

"Hello young man," the owner said. "And who is that pretty lady guiding you to the dance floor?"

"Hi," she said as she laughed at his comment and his wink. They had passed the door test—tipsy but not belligerent. Once inside the front door she turned him to the left and stopped at the kitchen area.

"How about some service," she hollered out so her best friend who was working the counter would notice her and the guy hanging around her neck.

"Well," her friend said as she grabbed a towel and wiped the counter, "just look at you two."

"We need a couple of Sloppy Joes and a cup of coffee," she said.

"Coming right up."

The kitchen also opened up on the dance floor side of the hall. It was dark on the hall side but brightly lit on the lobby side so it was easier for folk on the inside to see folks on the outside. She made it a point to stand in the most brightly-lit area so anyone who was looking would see the guy she was with. He was Mr. Everything at high school and tonight, she was his guide to a life beyond the classroom.

"Here ya go," her friend said as she put the two napkin wrapped Sloppy Joes on the counter and tried to hand him the cup of hot black coffee. He reached out for the coffee but his hand missed it to the right as he made a gentle grab at her breast.

"Need cream?" she asked in response to his move.

He grinned sheepishly, pulled his arm from around his adopted date's neck, and rested his elbows on the counter as he started to eat the sandwich. Meat fell to the counter as his lack of coordination was starting to show. She knew he was dangerously close to going over the sober hill and her chances for something "meaningful" were slipping away unless she could get coffee, sandwiches, and dancing to work in her favor.

"Let's go dance," she said as she turned his head toward her and away from the remains of the second sandwich that was falling apart in his hands. She wiped his hands and put his arm around her neck and headed for the small hallway that lead to the dance floor. A railing separated the hallway and on the right side was a window where you paid to enter the dance floor area. A security person stood at the end of the hallway and watched to make sure your stamp of payment, now on the top of your hand, showed up under a black light. No stamp, out!

The stage was on the far end and the two sides were lined with wooden, unpadded booths capable of seating four large people, or depending on age from four to ten kids. There was another group of booths located up stairs above the bar and the kitchen. She wanted to take him up there but he was in no condition to climb the steps. That was a serious business area and most local kids had absolute instructions to never go up there. It was dark up there. The polka band broke into a slow waltz as they entered the dance floor.

"Come on," she said, "let's dance."

"I can't dance."

"I'll teach ya."

"I feel sick."

"Put your arms around my neck and hold on," she said as she turned and threw his arms over her shoulders. "You'll be fine. Now just follow me."

She slowly guided him into the crowded dance floor, spending most of her efforts trying to hold him up so he wouldn't slump on someone's wife or girlfriend. That could cause a fist to fly and that could turn the dance into the fight of the week. She waved at friends as they stumbled around the floor. The word would soon be out. She was with him. Were they seeing each other? By morning, the rumor mill would be wild with speculation.

"I feel sick," he said as he rested his chin on her shoulder. He was starting to drool and his eyes were drifting in and out of focus. She knew it was time to find a booth. She scanned the booths for an open spot. Finally she spotted the perfect place.

"Hi," she said to the couple sitting in one side of the booth, "can we join you?"

When it came to boys, especially this boy, no girl in the place offered her more competition than the one sitting in this booth. Most people thought the drunken boy on her arm was the perfect match for the girl in the booth.

"Is he drunk?" she asked.

"Just tired."

"He's not tired. He's drunk! I heard he went to Yankton and made his first buy."

"I didn't hear that," she said as she aimed his limp body at the booth. He fell into the booth and then rolled off the seat and onto the floor.

They both stared as he cuddled up under the table and tried to sleep.

"Did you get him drunk?"

"No," she said. "He just asked me to the dance."

"No he didn't."

"Well, he's with me isn't he?"

"He wouldn't know you from an oversized fence post right now."

"Excuse me, what did you say?"

By now, the other girl was leaning under the table trying to get a better look at the notorious hunk. She peered at him as he lay under the booth almost in a fetal position.

"If his parents find out you got him drunk, there will be hell to pay," she said as she looked up at his dance night date.

"And I wonder who spread a story like that? Sounds like just the job for a motor mouth like you."

"I'll get him some coffee," the other guy said as he quickly exited from the booth and the catfight.

"Thanks anyway," she said. "But we won't be staying."

She reached under the booth and grabbed him by the back of his belt and slid him out on the dance floor. She picked him up and put his arm around her neck and hauled him away. His eyes opened halfway and drool was still coming from his mouth. His blond hair was messed and shooting out in all directions. He tried to rub his right eye with the palm of his right hand, now covered with sawdust and cigarette ashes.

"I feel sick," he mumbled.

"We're going," she said as she towed her prize catch off into the darkness and the crowd.

"What's that crap on the side of your car door?" his dad asked the next morning. "You get sick or something?"

"Bad pizza, Dad," he said as he rolled his aching head out of a wet pillow and tried to focus his bloodshot eyes. His head throbbed as he sat up on the edge of the bed. He looked at his stained shirt. It smelled. His room smelled. He smelled.

"What the hell is that on the side of your neck?"

"What do you mean, Dad?"

"Looks like a scratch or a bruise."

"I don't know, Dad."

"Well get up and get that car cleaned up in a hurry," his dad ordered. "I don't want your mother worried about you staying up half the night getting sick on bad pizza."

"OK Dad."

"Where were you anyway?"

"Dancing, Dad."

"Dancing?" his dad asked as he looked at his stained and bad smelling boy, "that must have been some dance."

"It was Dad," he said as he rubbed traces of sawdust from his eyes.

He watched his dad turn and walk away without saying another word.

The Day
That Kennedy Came

◆

There was big news going around town. The young senator from Massachusetts, now seeking the highest office in the land, was coming to Nebraska to campaign in the Nebraska primary. He was going to motorcade through the state and he was coming to Hartington. He was going to give a speech on the old track and football field down in front of the public high school.

"Dad," the young son said as he opened the door to his dad's Ford® dealership showroom, "did you hear that Senator is coming here to give a speech?"

"You mean Senator Kennedy?"

"Yea, Dad," the boy said, "that guy. Are you going to vote for him?"

"I don't know," his father said. "Politics is really something you shouldn't talk about."

"Why not, Dad?"

"Well, people have different views when it comes to politics," his dad explained. "People can get riled up about that kind of stuff. Religion is the same way."

"You mean like being Lutheran instead of Catholic?"

"Like that."

"So I shouldn't talk about politics and religion?"

"I didn't say that," his father said as he tried to figure out a way out of the discussion. "Just keep in mind that those two subjects can cause arguments. Just be cautious what you say and who you say it too."

"I think I understand that, Dad," the boy said as he picked up a Ford Times®, "so who are you going to vote for?"

"I don't know."

"Are you going to listen to his speech when he comes?"

"I don't know."

"Are you going down to the high school at least?"

"I don't know."

"You aren't really that interested in politics are you, Dad?"

"No," his dad said, "I don't suppose I am."

"Then why did you run for mayor all of those years?"

"My friends wanted me to run and there were some things I wanted to get done."

"Like what?"

"Like paving the streets so people wouldn't have muddy roads when it rained and snowed."

"Well maybe this Senator has some things he wants to get done."

"Maybe so."

"Why don't you go with me to hear his speech then?"

"Ok, we'll go," his dad said, "I guess you can't be a good voter if you don't hear what they have to say."

"Do you believe politicians, Dad?"

"Not all of them."

"Do you think you will believe this guy?"

"We'll see."

His son was excited as the Saturday morning came. Everything was ready for the Senator's arrival. The scouts hung the American flags on all of the Main Street light poles. The flag display was usually reserved for major holidays. A special speaker's platform had been constructed on the football field. Kennedy for President posters hung all over town on anything that could hold a staple. The boy walked around the streets and listened to the farm folks and city folks talk about the upcoming event.

"He's Catholic," a lady said to her friend as they stood outside of the People Store. "If he gets elected, he will have to take orders from the Pope."

"That absurd," her friend argued, "he is his own man. Just look at his record as senator."

"Well I don't know, I can't vote for a Catholic."

The boy wandered through the growing crowds as the clock moved toward eleven. The parade, or at least the caravan of cars, was suppose to arrive at eleven in the morning but rumor was spreading. The caravan was late.

"I ain't waiting to hear this stuff," a farmer told his wife as they headed for the car. "I have chores to do and no time to waste listening to some guy tell us a bunch of lies about what he is going to do for farmers."

"How do you know what he says will be a lie?" his wife asked.

"He's a politician, ain't he?"

"So?"

"Well, they all lie."

"Excuse me sir," the boy said as he looked at the farmer, "My dad was the mayor here and he didn't lie."

The farmer stopped for a second and shifted the bags of groceries to get a better look at the boy.

"Your dad is an exception. I would vote for him for President," the farmer said as he brushed the boy's blond hair.

It was time. There wasn't a parking place in town and folks walked down Main Street to the football field. Finally, a state trooper's car turned the corner followed by a number of other cars. Senator Kennedy was in Hartington.

The boy raced down the street to his dad's Ford® garage, opened the door and ran up to the parts counter

"Dad, he's here!" the excited boy hollered as he ran back to the front door, opened it and looked up the street.

The boy's dad looked up from the parts book and finally started to show a little interest. He didn't say anything but walked slowly to the front door where his son stood with his eyes focused up Main Street.

Since none of the cars were convertibles, it wasn't really clear to the boy which car would hold the Senator. As the cars passed by, the boy could only rely on the pictures he had seen to really be sure that he could see him.

"Dad, which car is he in?"

"I don't know," his dad said as the cars went by at ten miles and hour. "I don't even know if I could recognize him if I saw him."

"He has a lot of hair, Dad. It looks all messed up."

About mid-way in the procession, a car passed with the window rolled down. In the back seat sat a man, pitched ahead a little bit, looking carefully out his window at the storefronts in the little town.

"There he is!" the boy hollered out as he jumped and started to wave. The boy felt a lightning bolt go through him as the Senator's eyes met his. The Senator smiled and waved at the boy.

"It's him Dad!" the boy said as he turned and pulled on his dad's arm. "He waved at me just like I was his friend or something. Did you see him, Dad? It's the President!"

"He's not the President yet my boy," his dad said as he turned and walked back to the parts counter.

The crowd filled the football field to hear the Senator's speech. One of the local hosts gave him a commemorative plate from the recent big seventy-five year celebration.

"It's ahr, very nice to be with yur and have a chance to breathe, ah, this fresh country air of Nebrasker," he started his speech as he took a deep breath. "Ahr...hogs."

"He's funny, Dad," the boy said as he laughed at the joke and looked up at his dad.

He talked of challenge. He talked about believing in a nation of unlimited promise. He made the farmers feel just as important at the people in the city. He talked about the value of strong faith and family. He might win big in Hartington.

As usual, study hall was quiet and boring. There was a front door and a rear door in the big study hall on the third floor of the high school building. No one usually came in the rear door unless it was the principle wanting to pull someone out for some type of discussion. It was very unusual for the rear door toopen. This day it did.

Students turned because of the unusual noise. Standing at the back door of the study hall was the school janitor. He stood in the open door with his oiled dust mop and was visibly upset. He said only five words.

"The President has been shot," he said. The students had heard the Pearl Harbor news of their time.

By the time the teenage boy got home, the television was already blaring away with trusty Walter Cronkite at the news desk.

"Pres..a..dent John FFF Kennedy has been aaasasassinated in Dallassss, Texas." By evening, the now gathered family was introduced to other facts. It happened in a motorcade. The Governor of Texas was also shot. The motorcade was "whisked" away to Parkland Hospital. The President died shortly after one in the afternoon. There appeared to only be one assassin. The shots came from the sixth floor of a building called the Texas School Book Depository. The President's body would be flown back to Washington that night. Something had happened at a local movie theater and a Dallas policeman had been shot. Someone had been arrested.

Finally night came along with blurry black and white live pictures from Dallas. The President's plane, Air Force One, waited in stillness. A funeral coach arrived with the remains of the President. An honor guard carried the flag covered casket to a large lift at the back of the plane. Slowly, the device lifted the honor guard and the casket up to the back door of the plane. The casket soon disappeared into the plane.

Almost in a whisper, reporters talked back and forth with each other tying to tell people what people could see for themselves. The family watched as the big jet taxied away into the suddenly lonely sky. A few hours later the plane landed at Andrews Air Base in Washington. It wasn't long before the television audience was shown a black and white a photograph of the new President of the United States, Texan Lyndon Johnson. He stood solemnly, with one of his hands raised and the other hand on the Bible, being sworn into office. Jackie stood in the background.

"Oh poor Jackie," the boy's mother said as she wiped a few tears from her eyes. "Oh poor Jackie and those little kids."

The boy's dad didn't say a word as he watched Walter fill in the latest news about the man arrested and accused of firing the fatal shots. He, along with his sons and the rest of the country were starting to learn about a man named Lee Harvey Oswald.

The boy went to the kitchen and looked out into the night. He noticed how quiet the little town had become. Nothing was going on. No traffic. No people on the streets. Businesses closed.

During the following days, the only sound heard was sound of drums. For days everyone heard the same sound of drums. "Bump bump bump, da da da bump bump bump, da da da bump bump bump, da da da bump bump da bump."

They watched as a country moved their leader to the White House, and then to the Capitol, and then watched the slow and silent parade of stillness interrupted only by the piercing voice of the honor guard commander as he barked out orders and put precision into focus. They listened to the sound of dirges and the Navy Hymn as the casket moved from place to place.

"He looked right at me, Dad," the boy said as his eyes filled with tears. "He looked right at me."

He brought enough charisma and enough of a vision to win Hartington hearts and votes. He looked these people right in the eyes and sent a lightning bolt of excitement right into their hearts. He smiled at them. He waved at them. He promised a bright future and told everyone America was going to the moon.

"What gonna happen now, Dad?"

"I don't know but President Johnson will do a good job," his dad said. "He has a lot of experience."

"But he's pretty old, Dad."

"No son, President Kennedy was just very young."

"It's for you," the boy's mother said as she held the phone towards him.

"Hello," the boy said. "Sure I can do that. Tomorrow at 11:00. OK. Bye."

"The VFW and wants me to play taps at a memorial service for the President on Sunday morning," he told his parents. That wasn't an unusual request because he was one of the regular bugle boys used for military service. Any veteran could choose to have a military service complete with VFW color guard, firing squad, and a bugler playing taps. He played taps several times in all kinds of weather from hot sun to ten degrees below zero freezing cold. He finally learned how to make his horn sing rather than just play the mournful song as the sound filtered through the countryside.

On early Sunday morning, the old veterans presented the colors, fired the three volleys from the seven rifles, and the boy raised his horn and let the sad sound of taps cut the stillness of the small town air.

"What happened?" he asked as he entered the house and heard the TV set blaring. Walter brought the new. A Dallas businessman, Jack Ruby, had shot the assassin.

"Oh my, will this ever end!" the boy's mom questioned as she stood and watched the pictures of Oswald's final seconds. "What is going on in this country?"

"Dad, is this how politics is going to be?" the boy asked.

"I hope not, at least not in this country. I never thought it could happen in this country."

The boy sat down on a footstool next to his dad and watched the camera switch from the honor guard, to the mourners, and back to the casket in the Capitol Rotunda.

"God bless you Mr. President," he said. "Good bye my friend."

Working for Dad

———————◆———————

If it wasn't a drought ruining things, a new twist on the farm program
did. Whether it was cars or almost anything else, good years never
seemed to run in strings. It was tough to keep up with the expense of
new technology, new taxes, and used cars that were hardly ever low
mileage and always rode hard and put away squeaking. Folks wanted,
and needed top dollar for their trade-ins and this Ford® dealer knew it.
This little dealership's used car lot was full of a bunch slingers—worn
out cars that nobody but a school kid with a fresh driver's license could
appreciate.

Miller Motor operated in the same spot since it opened in 1912. It
was a storefront garage with three big blue doors facing Main Street.
The showroom, which faced the street, had full floor to ceiling glass and
enough space to hold two cars if you could squeeze them through the
doorway that faced the shop area. As the Ford® line grew bigger and
wider, the showroom door, built to let a Model T scoot though, was
getting to be a problem. One slip and the narrow doorway would
scratch the door of the new Ford®.

"Arrughhh Got amit!" came the holler from the owner's office when he
heard the little squeak caused by the scarping of a shiny new car door as it
collided with the wooden door frame at a speed of one inch per hour.

At the back of the showroom was the parts department. There were
lines of shelves which held every nut, screw and bolt Ford® ever made.

If the needed part wasn't in the front part of the parts department, it was probably in the unheated huge storage room behind the parts department. Need a wiring harness for a Model A? Miller Motor had it. How about a quarter panel for a 1950 Ford® convertible? Miller Motor had it. Do you need a short block for a forty-nine flat head? Miller Motor had it. The inventory contained tons of obsolete, money-hogging, old Ford® parts that dated back almost as long as Ford® did. The parts area was running out of room trying to keep up with the new and trying to store all of the old. The Ford® roadman wasn't the least bit interested in buying back the old obsolete parts. New Model-T parts often went to the city dump.

Mr. Miller knew his parts numbers like no one else in the business. If a customer walked in and asked for a carburetor spring for a 1968 390 engine, the knowledgeable dealer would be saying C8AZ something before he would open the parts book catalog which was always on the top of the parts counter. If he couldn't instantly find it, he went back to a special small metal table which was full of 5X7 inch inventory cards and got the exact inventory on hand and the exact location.

"Arrughhh Got amit!" came a frequent muffled sound from the back.

"Jerome," he said to his parts man, "this card is not right. It's out of date. We show three on hand and there are none in the rack." Not surprising after fifty years of business.

Jerome, the parts man, customer service man, door opener, door closer, occasional wrecker driver, snow shoveler, was the kind of employee every boss should have. He stayed with Mr. Miller in the bar business and came back with him to the Ford® business when Mr. Miller's brother, who ran the garage, passed away.

He trained Jerome in his style. After all, a good parts man is not an easy employee to come by. He carefully trained Jerome in Ford's® numbering system, how to read the parts books, how to use and read the new fangled micro film system, how to read the dealer's shorthand, how to order enough of the right stuff, how to not order any of the soon-to-be-obsolete stuff.

Jerome was a big, strong friendly guy and got things done at top speed which occasionally caused a small problem. He liked a good story and loved to kid the customers. He also knew which ones would require dead seriousness. Jerome had to learn the complex parts system, day by day, part by part, and order by order.

"Arrughhh Got amit!" Apparently replacement seat padding for a Falcon® didn't look like such a good idea after all.

The garage had good help, committed to quality work at a fair price, and most of them had been there forever—from greasy little pups to front office people.

Gildersleeve was the top salesman. He stood about five-foot tall, had a funny and loud, long lasting laugh that was infectious. He had short arms, legs, and small hands. He had a twinkle in his eye. He loved a good practical joke. He was never angry. He knew everybody in the county and was a tick or two to the plump side. His first name was Ted but most folks just called him Gildersleeve. In those days, you took the car or truck to the farmer rather than have the farmer come to town to see you. A new car could come back with plenty of interesting smelling mud on the new carpet. "We'll take her," were the sweetest words a country Ford® dealer could hear.

Ted spent his time driving all over the country roads selling cars, selling Ford® farm machinery, and driving families for funerals, a tradition the Miller family always offered people in Hartington and farm country. Many of those folks were not be able to buy a new car, but their family got to ride in one if a family member had dropped dead trying to make a living in the hilly, often dry, corn country.

Ted visited from sun up to sun down. He was visiting in the showroom. He was visiting on the street. He was visiting in the coffee shop. He was visiting at church. Ted knew what was going on. He was also a volunteer fireman as were a number of the men in the garage.

When the fire whistle sounded, Miller Motor went temporarily out of business while all of the mechanics raced out the front doors and back downstairs body shop doors and ran around the corner to take driving command of the fire trucks. One was a trusty 1951 Ford® pumper that always made it to the fire, and the other was an old forties vintage International® which often didn't make it to the stop sign at the top of the hill. The fire whistle signaled the start of the "fittest of the fattest race." Some folks were amazed half of the firemen didn't drop dead of a heart attack trying to be first at the firehouse.

All of the parking in front of Miller Motor was angular, with no parking in front of the three big blue garage doors. A customer could pull up in front of one of the doors, honk the car horn, and Jerome would push the one of the three buttons to open right door. The customer then drove inside and Jerome would be waiting with clip board and work ticket. The ten minute oil change and filter was born at Miller Motor almost fifty years ago. Give the grease man thirty minutes and he could undercoat a car.

The grease man was the skinny guy at Miller Motor and didn't mind the drippy oil, the grease, or the thawing snow, mud, and water running down his arms and into his shirt sleeves as long as there were plenty of grease rags around. On a good busy Saturday, his doors were opening faster than gang members grabbing merchandise on riot day. The large gas heaters, mounted high above the shop were also going full time as the big doors bounced open and shut.

"Arrughhh Got amit!" mumbled Mr. Miller. He knew what it cost to heat the garage and the Main Street of Hartington in the wintertime. "Were you guys born in a barn? Close the doors!"

Miller Motor had two mechanics going full blast all day long. They overhauled engines. They did tune-ups. They aligned front ends. They solved car problems and sent Hartington drivers out the door happy and safe. Most of all, they did it without the advantage of the high tech analysis machines that most auto service companies have today. Mr. Miller didn't have the money to outfit the garage with the latest equipment and no one could really be sure if that early group of car fixers would have used all of that high tech stuff in the first place. They used ears, eyes, experience, and tenacity to get problems solved and believed the best computer in the shop was the one located directly above the blue work shirts which had the Miller Motor name on the back of them. Once in a while, they also got so cocky they knew what color cars to order.

"Arrughhh Got amit!" Mr. Miller mumbled. "I'll do the car ordering around here."

At the back of the main shop floor, right next to the front-end machine, was a dark stairway, which lead to the basement level of the garage. At the bottom of the stairway was a door which lead to the messy, dirty, dust covered, smelly, body shop. The Main Street side of the garage was really the second floor to the body shop guys. The body shop opened onto the alley. Main Street was built on the top of the hill and the garage was plugged into the side of the hill.

Miller had three sons. The two older boys, both teenagers, worked on the weekends and sometimes after school. Miller's youngest son tested cars after school, driving up and down Main Street until it was time to go home for dinner. Mr. Miller nicknamed this kid "Dizzy" because of his round and round driving pattern on Main Street. The middle son worked in the body shop. The mechanics named this boy "Junior" since he had the same first name as his dad. The older boy spent his time in the showroom, meeting customers, and occasionally driving the wrecker to help push start cars or to recover wrecked cars when the police called for assistance.

"Now Junior," the bodyman said as he handed the boy a roll of masking tape, "make sure you cover the chrome and make sure the tape doesn't touch the finish. If the tape touches the finish, it will cause a paint run and that just ain't a gonna happen in this place."

"Like this?" the boy said as he pulled a couple of inches of tape off of the roll and tried to meticulously follow the instructions from his boss.

"Stand aside," the bodyman boss said. "Like this," he said as he took the roll of tape, pulled out a couple of feet and covered the entire car length chrome strip in just seconds.

The garage was a teenager's dream come true. There was a constant supply of new cars and used cars, a good supply of quick-clamp dealer license plates and a big and powerful wrecker. In Miller Motor's case, the wrecker was a large twin boom job.

"This car is a demonstrator," Mr. Miller said as he talked about the shiny new car he had just driven home. "I don't want you knotheads driving it. We use it to demonstrate to customers, not haul a bunch of kids around town."

The boys had heard the new demonstrator warning before and knew the main points of the speech by heart. New car. Knotheads couldn't drive it. It was going to be a demonstrator only—used to show other prospective buyers how the car performed and not how sexy a knothead could look as he "tooled" around town during the late evening hours. The older brother and Junior understood the new demonstrator was hands-off for at least two weeks. That was usually the amount of time necessary until Mr. Miller got used to the new car. After two weeks, it was just another demonstrator. First come first served.

Normally, the demonstrators were four door Ford® sedans. The older boys were never very excited about driving the demonstrators for that reason. They would just as soon go to the used car lot, located a couple of blocks away from the garage and slip a dealer plate on a more sporty used car. Junior's favorite was a 1959 Ford® two door hardtop with a stick shift and a 390 engine. If it was a new demonstrator, on the other hand, "Dizzy" was driving it.

No one will ever know what came over the boy's dad. Maybe a mechanic had bitched once too often about Baffin blue four doors, or maybe he just wanted to live it up a little. But, one day the new car transport truck pulled up in front of Miller Motor with a couple of Baffin blues four-doors, a desert tan four-door, and a white Mercury®

two door hardtop with black leather interior and the latest stereo system with eight track tape deck. Half the town noticed when the sporty Mercury® followed the Baffin blue and the desert tan off the transport and into door number one of the Miller Motor Company. The two older sons were skeptical as the transport driver headed for the showroom with the delivery paperwork for their dad to sign. The truck driver went into the front office and their dad soon came out to inspect the cars. Either the transport driver had off loaded the snazzy Mercury® at the wrong dealership or Ford® had shipped an unordered unit—a sure"Arrughhh Got amit!" or Mr. Miller had actually ordered this beautiful, hot new Mercury®.

"Look, he's actually checking it for damage," the older son pointed out to his younger brother.

"Junior," a mechanic hollered from across the shop, "your dad didn't actually order that Mercury® did he? It isn't blue!" he said as he laughed.

They watched as their dad and trusty Jerome walked around the car looking for damage that could often happen on the trip from the Mercury® plant to Nebraska. Finally, Mr. Miller signed for the Mercury® and the driver got back into the transport and started the engine. There was not even a hint of "Arrughhh Got amit!"

"I don't believe it," the older son said. He knew which cars were on order or had been sold. He didn't know a thing about this one.

"Put thirty-four on that white Mercury® and clean it up," he said to his middle son. The instructions we're crystal clear. He wanted Junior to put license plate 13-DLR-34 on the new Mercury®. That was Mr. Miller's demonstrator plate so his instructions meant that the Mercury® was not only ordered by him, but also meant that it would be a demonstrator. At the dinner table that night, the conversation was predictable.

"This Mercury® is a demonstrator. I don't want you knotheads to put a lot of miles on it." The older sons clearly understood it would be two weeks before they could drive the new Mercury®. Dizzy had other plans.

After dinner, Mr. Miller decided to drive to the country club. It was raining so he decided to drive the Econoline® pickup instead of the new Mercury®. The older son went out with a friend. Junior decided to watch television.

The rain came down in a steady pour. The boy's mom was in the kitchen doing dishes and other things when the phone rang.

"Millers," she politely answered. "What!" Aaahhhhhaaa! The brand new Mercury®? Aaaahhhhhaaaa! Come hear," she hollered to her T.V watching son. The boy dashed to the kitchen where he found his anxious mother holding out the phone to him. She looked very worried.

"Talk to your brother," she said. "He took the new Mercury ® and he is stuck in the mud!"

Dizzy had taken the snazzy new Mercury® and slid into the ditch on his way to the bowling alley located about a half mile outside of the city limits. The bowling alley road had recently been graded and re-graveled. Mix new grading, new gravel, and a good rain and that means mud. Lots of mud.

"Where are you now?" Junior asked.

"At the bowling alley," Dizzy answered.

"Are you OK?"

"Yes. Just muddy and wet."

"OK, stay there. I'll get the wrecker and come out."

"Where's Dad?" Dizzy asked.

"He's at the Country Club."

In his father's eyes, Junior had become a trustworthy and responsible employee. As a result, his dad had given him his own garage key. There was absolutely no need for him to go out to the country club and ask his dad for the key, and come up with the right answer as to why he needed it. Junior also loved to drive the old wrecker and pick up all forms of vehicles, in all kinds of weather, at all hours of the day or night. Junior and the older son could safely pull a car out of the ditch and tow it back to town without much of a problem. They could even hoist a cow that couldn't quite hoof it out of the way in time so the farmer could at least salvage the meat from a four hoof, four wheel collision.

Junior grabbed his Miller Motor shop coat, a sure sign that he was off on official business. He laced up his trusty waterproof hunting boots, which was a sure sign he was headed for door number three where the big six ton, two boom, red with flashing red light wrecker waited patiently for just such an emergency. A wrecker call really got Junior's adrenaline going so he was always in a little bit of a hurry even as he threw open the back door and almost knocked his dad down as he was coming into the house.

"Where the hell are you going?" his father asked.

"Wrecker call, Dad," he said as he tried to avoid eye contact and reach his '59 Ford® without any further questions. He thought answers would be better if they came from his mother a little later.

"Who is dumb enough to be out driving in this," his dad said as he looked back at the driving rain and entered the house.

"Your youngest son got the new Mercury® stuck in the mud out by the bowling alley," his wife said.

"Arrughhh Got amit!" the dad shouted. "Wait a minute," he hollered at his middle son who had his car started and was almost ready to leave. " I'll go with you! Arrughhh Got amit!"

"I can get it OK, Dad," Junior hollered back through the rain. "Stay there."

"No wait, I'm going along."

In a couple of minutes, he came out of the back door wearing a golf rain jacket and a pair of zipped up rubber overshoes. The garage was only three blocks from the family house so they were there in a matter of minutes.

"I'll open the door and you get it out," his dad said as they pulled up in front of the garage.

The shop floor lights soon flickered on and blue door number three started to open. There was the boy's pride and joy, like a great horse, ready to go for a run. He jumped up on the running board of the old truck and hopped inside the cab. He turned on the key and stomped the starter button the floor. Instantly, the 1946 Ford® truck came to life, and with a few quick punches of the gas pedal, the garage now had a smell of gas and a little cloud of black smoke as the old Ford® flathead V-8 was ready for a run. There wasn't a wrecker in town that had the pull of this one and the boy loved to be the one to command her power.

The old wrecker had straight gears in the transmission. In order to get a nice, clean, no grind shift, the boy had to "double clutch" between each gearshift. Push the clutch in. Let it out. Push the clutch in again. Shift to reverse. Give it a little gas. Let it out. Slowly the big truck moved out of the garage and onto Main Street. Young teenager and old truck were one.

He watched as his dad punched the button on the wall and door number three started coming down. His dad disappeared for a second into the showroom and then came out the front door, locked it, and got into the passenger side of the wrecker. The boy pulled the light switch and the big truck came to life like a Christmas tree. Five bullet-shaped amber clearance lights lit up on the top of the cab. Two red turn signals lit up on the top of the boom. As a matter of habit, he also gave his favorite power switch a pull. Whoosh. Whoosh. Whoosh. The high powered red light on the top of boom was in perfect working order and throwing its powerful beam in a circle you could see for blocks in town, or for miles in the country.

"Arrughhh Got amit! Shut that damn thing off," his dad ordered. "We'll have every knothead in town following us."

"OK Dad," Junior said as he brought his excitement down a level or two.

Wreckers and fire trucks leaving town drew a crowd. The rain was still coming down so a good portion of the local Dizzy brigade had parked for the night. The windshield wiper had its hands full as it cleared a semi circle in front of the young driver. Junior took a two-handed death grip on the steering wheel of the old truck as it bounced through the water filled ruts of the road leading to the bowling alley. The high back red sides with "Miller Motor" painted on it made sure none of the assorted chains would fall out onto the road as the old truck bounced along. A smooth ride in a big truck was still some time off in the Ford® engineering future.

"Where is he?" his dad asked.

"The car?"

"No, Dizzy."

"He's at the bowling alley."

"Is he hurt?"

"No, just muddy and wet."

He slowed down and shifted into a lower gear because he could feel the weight of the truck sinking into the soft earth. The engine was starting to puff a little harder as the big dual rear tires cut a set of ruts into what the county had hoped would be a new smooth, stone cover expressway. His younger brother told him the Mercury® was just off the edge of the road on the other side of Mrs. Cobbler's place. As they passed Mrs. Cobbler's farm lane, the truck headlights lit up the side of a white, very muddy looking car.

"Arrughhh Got amit!"

There was his dad's new pride and joy demonstrator, rear end off the ground and front end at a rather nasty angle into a ditch filled with muddy water. The water was almost over the hood of the awesome car. By now, the wrecker was barley creeping along. There was no way he could turn the truck around and get the business end to the back end of the Mercury® on this bean soup excuse of a new road.

"I'll have to go to the intersection before I can turn around Dad, or I'll be in the ditch on the other side."

No comment so the plan was approved. Junior drove on by the stuck car to the intersection and turned the truck around and headed back. Since he had the entire road now blocked, it was "whoosh-whoosh-whoosh" time. He pulled the switch out and watched as the red light reflected against everything in its path for as far as the eye could see. God did he love the sight of that red light bouncing off poles, barns, signs, weeds, cows, and anything else.

"I'll hook it up," his dad said. It was obvious his dad wanted to have a look at the sinking Mercury®. The boy flipped another panel switch and instantly, the floodlights on the back of the boom and under the back of the truck, came on and flooded the scene with light. The new Mercury® looked just like the Titanic, bow down-stern up, going down into a sea of muddy water and old corn stalks.

"Be careful Dad, the shoulder is soft."

The warning came too late. His dad had just made the discovery for himself and slid down the newly graded clay gumbo mud bank into the rising sea of cold dirty green water.

"Arrughhh Got sssssssssshhhhhhhhh!" The boy had never heard the sound of human steam before.

By now, the flashing red light had attracted a little attention. A car came down the road and stopped. A boy got out of the passenger side. It was Dizzy and he was just in time to see his father crawl out of the ditch full of mud and water.

"Go on home," the father order.

Dizzy looked at Junior and was out of there like a jackrabbit that had wandered into a coyote family reunion around supper time.

"It's hooked up," he said to Junior as he got back into the wrecker's cab. He was soaked from head to foot and covered with brown mud. "Pull it out and let's get the hell out of here."

The soggy dad now trusted his wrecker running boy to finish the job and they were soon on their way back to town—muddy new Mercury® in tow.

Northeastern Nebraska mud has to come off quick or it dries hard enough to make a sod house wall. A steam cleaner was the best tool to get the mud off the transmission and the engine. Junior fired up the steam cleaner and his dad went home.

Junior was under that muddy mess for almost an hour and a half and was covered with mud from head to toe when he finally got home.

"Take off those muddy clothes," his mom said as she met him at the door with a towel. His dad was in the family room watching TV.

"Where's my wonderful little brother?" he asked his mom as he stripped to his skivvies.

"He hasn't come home yet." she whispered. "Your father is a little upset. Oh mercy, mercy."

Not long after his nice long hot shower, he heard the back door open. He knew it was face the music time for Dizzy.

"Should I get my horn and play 'Taps'?" he asked his mom as he watched his little brother sit down on the footstool in front of their father.

"I'm sorry," he heard his little brother say. The boy looked down at the floor as he waited for his dad to speak.

"Did you learn anything?"

"Yes," came the sheepish reply. "I am not that good of a driver to be out in those conditions. I am sorry I got your new car all dirty, Dad."

"OK. Why don't you hit the bed."

"OK? Why don't you hit the bed? Is that all that he gets after I spent half my night cleaning up his mess?" Junior asked his mom. "He gets to take his nice clean and dry body up to a nice warm bed. How can he get away with this?"

"Take another look," she told him. "Maybe someday you'll have a son and hope more than anything that he'll always come home safe."

"Arrughhh Got amit!" Junior said as he grabbed the dog and went off to bed.

Hello Old Friend

◆

He opened the car door, got out and started to walk across the grass. When he reached his old friend, he sat down on the grass next to him. "Hey, it's been a long time," he said.

It was the end of May and there was a hint of thunderstorms starting to form in the West.

"Boy, this is Nebraska isn't it. Sultry and hot."

"Remember when we first met? I told everyone in school that I was going to kick your ass. Never saw you. I just heard you were a nice guy and I didn't want you to take my friends away. I was the top dog and you were nipping at my grand heals."

"And, I challenged you to a fight the first day. You didn't blink or flinch. You just calmly followed me over to the courthouse lawn where the big fight was going to take place. All you wanted to know is if we were going to fist fight or wrestle. I think we rolled around for a minute or two and that was it. 'See ya tomorrow,' you said. You could care less who won that fight and I was scared to death you were going to pound me into the ground."

He looked back at the clouds building in the West. "Bet we have some storms tonight. Seems like we always do this time of year and especially this weekend. I wonder if the band will parade?"

"Remember the first time we saw Miss Stone? You didn't say anything about how big she was. The rest of us did. But not you. Oh no! If your mom would have heard you say a bad word about a teacher, you would have been herding cows from four in the morning until midnight."

"Your folks had a nice place. All of those building were always in top-notch shape and painted. It looked really neat sitting up there on the side of the hill. Your dad always had the weeds cut down and the yard mowed. I can't remember a farm as neat and tidy as that one."

"Remember when I spent that weekend with you during calving time? That one cow was ready to give birth and instead of us running back to the house to get your dad, I had to jump in the corral and get a better look. You almost swallowed that shoot of broam grass you had sticking out the side of your mouth. And that cow wanted nothing to do with a city kid like me, hell in pain or not, she was up on her feet with the calf coming out of the birth canal. I had never seen anything like that. And when she fell back on her side, we both knew that calf was dead."

"Your family, especially your dad was always so nice to me. He should have run me out for spooking that cow."

"We did a lot of things together, didn't we? Remember when Miss Stone said she was going to appoint a manager to take care of all of the new band uniforms? She appointed us. You would have been a student manager with me for the basketball team if you didn't have so many chores to do at home. I really don't know how you farm kids got all that stuff done and still had time for band and in your case, football."

"Remember those two-a-days in late August? We may have been better off just sitting under a tree sipping on cold cherry Coke®. Never won a game. For three years, we never won a game. That coach cussed at us and hollered until the veins in his neck stood out like a water hose covered with skin. My dad said everyone downtown could hear him scream at us. And he was none to happy when his two prize linemen had to go play with the band before the game either."

"Heck, you liked band more than you ever liked football. You thought you were Tommy Dorsey with that trombone, or was it his brother that played the trombone? And sing, remember when Miss

Stone said you could sing like an angel. I laughed for two days. An angel. My buddy the big, blue-eyed Norwegian with cow manure on his boots was a singing angel. That was really funny. If she only knew some of the tricks you liked to play."

"What was the name of your sheriff uncle, the one that lived in Ceresco? I shit my pants that night that car came roaring up on me north of town with the siren and lights on. I threw six good beers into the ditch, and pulled over to the side of the road while that spotlight had my car all lit up. You started laughing and honking the horn and turned that spotlight on my six beers, shooting beer up into the air like Old Faithful. Just think what would have happened if the Cedar County Sheriff had just happened by about that time. We would have both gone to jail."

"You always did have a little adventure streak in you. I could dare you to do anything and if you had any kind of hint that you could outdo me, the deal was done. You won your fair share, that's for sure."

"But I beat you plenty of times, too. Football captain. Homecoming King. Student body president. I never beat you by more than a vote or two and you were always there right next to me. Except for music. I couldn't hold a candle to you when it came to music. Didn't matter what it was, you could whip me when it came to music. Remember the singing solos you used to do for Miss Stone at concerts? She was going to have me do one and that was almost enough for me to hop a freight and leave town. But not you. You just opened your mouth and let your tenor voice and perfect pitch capture every ear in the place. Even the reverend what's his name figured that one out."

"Remember the first time he used band members in church? We were up there in the balcony on Easter sunrise service and no one knew we were there. He came out into that dark church and hollered out, 'Christ has risen!' and we hit the horns to whatever that hymn was, remember, dah dah da duh dah dah dah dahhhhhh da dada da duh dada duh duh duh. Half of the old ladies in that place about jumped through their flowered hats. That was funny. I never had as much fun at church as I did with you."

"My mom always thought you were so polite and well mannered and so Christian. I was a little heathen compared to you. It was always a battle. Couldn't I spend more time at church like you did? If you only knew the grief you caused me."

"Ya know, it wouldn't have surprised me if you would have become a minister. I imagine it might have been a little tough on you being a prankster and all but I wasn't surprised when you decided to go to Midland Lutheran College. You always knew I was going to Nebraska and major in football watching. Did I tell you I tried out for the Cornhusker Marching Band? He stuck a sheet of music in front of me, and since I told him I could play a French horn as well as a coronet, he handed me the French horn. I honked away for about twenty notes and he said, 'that will be fine, check the list on Friday.' That was a long list but not long enough. You would have made it in a snap."

"I wish we had spent more time together that first year in college. We were only fifty miles apart and it would have been fun to have you come to Lincoln and play with the sinners. You would have liked my room-mate. His name was Tim and he was a farm kid from Lexington. Really a nice guy. Kind of a dark-haired version of you. Fun to be around. We were studying when I first heard. I didn't usually listen to the radio but I was that day. I almost didn't hear the story because I was studying economics. God did I hate that course. The announcer said, 'Midland College student drowns in sand pit lake during college party.' Tim looked up and said, 'hey, don't you have a buddy at Midland?"

"I said, 'ya, and if someone dared him to swim across a damn lake, he would do it.'

"The phone rang about the same time and Tim answered it. His face turned white and his eyes got real big as he handed the phone to me. It was my mom and she told me you had drowned."

"God I cried. I still do. No words ever worked to help me understand why you died. You were supposed to be forever with me. You were supposed to be there for me and I was supposed to be there for you. But somebody did dare you to swim across a lake. You couldn't swim any better than I could."

"Your funeral was one of my worst days. I remember looking at you in that casket. I remember hugging your poor mom and dad. They were devastated. So was my mom. She didn't know what to say to me. She just watched me stand there with those tears running down my face. I don't remember anything that was said on that day. All I remember is how cold that casket rail felt when we picked it up and we carried you out of the church and brought you here. I felt so alone standing over there while the minister committed your body to the ground. My shirt collar was wet when I got home. You would have laughed at that, huh. Your tough buddy standing in a cemetery crying himself dry."

"I went on of course and guess what I ended up doing? I became a pilot for a famous country singer. I flew his Learjet® and I can't tell you the number of times that I though about you sitting back there—you the famous country singer. You would have been, you know. You would have been something."

A raindrop hit him in the face as he got up on one knee and picked up a small garden hand spade and dug a small hole in front of the brown stone with the name Allen Grindvold carved in it.

"Guess I better get moving before the thunderstorms start moving in," he said as he looked back at the billowing white thunderheads claiming the dark blue Nebraska sky. "Maybe I will get this flower planted just in time for a nice gentle rain to get it watered just right."

He took a potted flower and placed it in the hole, pushed the dirt around the flower.

"I wonder if you get to see times like these, me planting a flower, or if you are busy singing and swooping around the heavenly skies," he said as he gathered the small spade and put it in the box. The raindrops were getting more frequent.

"Time for me to go," he said as he stood up and bowed his head. "I miss you but I can still hear you even after all of these years. Right here," he said as he lightly tapped the center of his chest. "Miss Stone was right you know. The heart is where the angels sing."

Looking for Bernard

◆

"There was a church down on the flat ground," his mother said as she stretched her arm out and pointed toward the rolling valley to the South. "Somebody bought it and moved it to town and made a house out of it. I remember the preacher had to walk up some steps to get to the pulpit and when there was a funeral, we all walked up here from the church."

He had been this place several times. He played cornet in the high school band and the local Veterans of Foreign Wars asked him, and one of his friends, to play taps on Memorial Day. The VFW started Memorial Day with sunrise services at Paragon Cemetery. His friend stood in the cemetery with the firing squad and honor guard and played taps after the three shot volleys. He walked down the dusty gravel road and played taps just after his friend finished. With proper distance, similar style, and no mistakes, his version sounded like an echo through the farm country hills. The echo was effective at Paragon because there was never a sound other than the wind blowing through the broam grass that lined the country roads. No traffic. No airplanes overhead. No voices. Not even a mooing cow. Paragon was the keeper of a pioneer past and only the chirp of a red-winged blackbird broke the rules of stillness.

"What's wrong Mom?" he asked.

"I want to find Bernard," she said.

"Who's Bernard?"

"He was my oldest brother and he died of whooping cough when he was just a little baby."

They spent most of the afternoon placing flowers on the graves of his Aunt Rebe and Uncle Jelly, his Uncle Bill, his grandfathers Sievert and Lee, and his grandmothers Andrena and Maude, and the very difficult stop for both of them, his dad. He even knew about his Uncle Leo who was killed in a farm house fire after he went back inside the burning farm house to try and save his first and only new pair of shoes. But, he had never heard about Bernard.

He unlatched the big gate and pushed it open. She headed straight for three big pine trees located at the top of the cemetery.

"Mom, watch out for the ground squirrel holes," he cautioned. Her eyesight was fading and she had trouble with cataracts. He worried she might trip and fall.

In front of those pines was a rusting flagpole with Old Glory fluttering in the sultry evening breeze. She walked up to a brown granite monument with the name Olson carved on it.

"These are my grandparents," she said.

"Is this Aunt Nellie?" he asked.

"Yes," she said as she stood next to him and looked at the stone. "She was so horribly stooped in those last days. Poor soul."

"I wonder if these are the Muck brothers who came to town on Saturday night when I was working at the grocery store," he said as he notice a row of smaller stones with Muck carved on each one. One brother drove a small tractor and the older brother sat on a high back chair in a wagon, pulled by the tractor. The wagon passenger had a long cane and tapped the tractor driver on the appropriate shoulder to let him know which way to turn.

"I was kind of scared of the one with the long pointy nose who wore that stained straw had with the sun visor sewn into the bill," he said.

"Do you remember Dad's new car showing when those two came in and stuffed all the free donuts into their denim overcoats?" she said as she grabbed his arm and smiled.

"Can you imagine what those smashed up donuts tasted like, Mom?"

Their odd ways were no longer visible or maybe even meaningful as their stories rested under matching brown granite stones. Only the stones let the world know that they had ever lived and died.

"Bernard's stone is a small white stone with a small lamb on top of it," she said as she started to search. Many of the stones suffered from the harsh winds of winter and the driving rains of spring. The letters, like the memories, were starting to fade.

"Mom, is this Bernard?"

Jens. B. Peterson. Born May 17. Died July 26. 1895. He lived a tad over two months. He could see the tears start to cloud his mother's eyes, as she stood silent in front of that little white stone with a lamb on the top. She folded her hands and stood in silent prayer. For a brief minute, the souls of brother and sister were together again.

"Give me my little spade, honey," she said as she put out her arm. He helped her kneel down. She dug a small hole in front of white lamb topped stone.

"Do you want the white one or the pink one?" he asked as he knelt next to her and pulled two of her prize peonies out of the bucket.

"I want to use some of both," she said as she carefully selected some of the huge blooms. She trimmed the stems and put them in small glass water filled jar and put the jar in the hole.

The wind had stopped blowing and the sun was slowly setting as it changed from its brilliant hot white to a more forgiving soft shade of gold. The flag hung limp on the rusting pole. Silence returned to the valley as the haze of summer softened the sky. He watched the soft golden light filter through the pine branches. It shined on his mother's face and the little white stone with the lamb on it. Brother and sister were together again.

"Thank you honey," she said as she put her hand on the back of his neck and pulled his face down toward her so she could kiss him on the cheek.

"I'm glad we came," she said as she strained to get up. They turned and walked arm and arm across the cemetery to the waiting car.

"Maybe next year we can bring some flowers and some glazed donuts," he said as he gave her a gentle hug and laughed.

A Snowy Day
for Mrs. Lubely*

◆

(*Pronounced Lube-a-lie)

She knew the snow had come. It started knocking at her bedroom window at three in the morning. Tink. Tink tink. Tink tink tink. She knew how the delicate crystals sounded as their journey to earth ended when they collided with the warm glass pane. She knew the morning would be bright, and for a while at least, the blanket of white would soften the busy world around her.

Her dawn always came at six. She had no need for an alarm clock. She awoke at six every morning even in the darkness of winter. She started her day as she always did, with a moment of prayer, a moment of reflection, and a moment of what the day could bring. She grabbed her cane, lifted herself from her bed, and carefully went to her bathroom and started a warm bath. Her knees hurt from arthritis but she pressed on. She would be better after a cup of tea and a hot bath.

As the tub filled, she went to the kitchen, filled the tea kettle with water and put it on her stove. From one of the crockery jars on her counter, she took a bag of tea and put it in her teapot. Soon both the tea water and her bath were hot. She looked through the living room now reflecting the morning sunshine and the bright white snow she knew had come during the night. It was hard for her to look at the snow; her right eye was almost blind from a cataract.

"So pretty," she said. Even through the blur of age, her memory could paint every detail of a snowy morning in her neighborhood.

If anyone were to ever see her in a robe, they would have to visit well before seven. By then, she was dressed in a silk dress, her ear rings on, a matching necklace, and a hint of rouge on her high cheekbones. Her silver gray hair didn't dare move out of place. She was ready for visitors should any decide to come.

She sat down at her kitchen table with her cup of tea. A touch of honey was in order on this morning. She had a slight chill from the wind as it challenged the door seals on her old house. Just as she finished her tea, the phone rang.

"Hello," she said.

"Hello Bun, yes isn't it beautiful outside."

"Oh no, I am not going out this morning."

"No, I have everything I need except for some groceries that should come out on delivery."

"Oh, the boy is already scooping the walk?"

"Well, whenever he has time to scoop my walk that will be fine."

"Thank you, you have a nice day, too."

"Bun, maybe when the snow gets cleared out a little, you can come over for tea."

"This afternoon around three would be just fine."

"Goodbye, Bun."

"Well," she said as she hung up the phone, "an unexpected pleasure." Her dear neighbor was coming for tea and her son would have the walks scooped soon. She knew the boy would do a good job.

The boy's dad was a stickler for getting the walks cleared as soon as the storm stopped and getting them cleared the entire width of the walk. There would be none of this meandering path stuff. The entire walk had to be cleared from grass side to grass side. All of the walks to the house, whether they had been used in the last twenty years or not, had to be completely cleared. The boy's mom made sure he chopped an equally wide path through that mound of ice the snowplows left out in front of the house when they barreled through town clearing the highway. That stuff was like shoveling rocks. Quite often, it was slushy and heavy and if the boy did not get at it soon, the mess would turn to Titanic killing ice. The boy's mother made sure that wouldn't happen

Mrs. Lubely pushed back her lace curtain and could see the boy scooping away the foot of new snow. His breath turned white as it came through the heavy scarf wrapped around the hood of his blue parka. He would be at her walk in an hour or so. She had time to bake a cake and have some hot chocolate ready for him when he reached her front door. She took her purse and looked for a crisp five-dollar bill and put it on the coffee table in her living room.

She was ready for the boy but he wasn't ready for the winter. The shovel stood like a sentry at the intersection of the two sidewalks. The footprints across the snow to the front door of the neighbor's house told the story. He was cold and tired and went in for a break.

"You have waited long enough. Get out there and get busy before Mrs. Lubely slips on the ice," his mom ordered.

"The snowplow is coming back, Mom," the son pleaded. "It won't do any good to scoop now. The snowplow will just fill the walk back up."

"Get out there this minute," she ordered. "The snowplow has already been by, I saw it half an hour ago."

Even the dog was loafing. She was hiding under the table next to the forced air duct where she could stay nice and toasty. The boy knew if he put his hands in kind of an "I'm gonna get ya" open choke hold, crouched a little bit, and approached the dog so the dog could see him; the dog would perk up and watch him—not as dog's best friend, but as dog's big threat. When the Scottie determined the threatening boy was close enough, she scrambled for protection under the mother's feet let out one loud bark causing the unsuspecting mother to jump about two feet in the air.

"Oh!" she hollered, "enough of that. Now get those walks cleared right now!"

The family Scottie had a proper Scottie trim—a big mustache and bottom third uncut. With this kind of cut, and with a large drift of fluffy snow, loafing boy could have a great time with the dog. He picked her up and tossed her into the top of the drift. She instantly sank into the soft fluffy snow and had to burrow and jump her way out of it. As a result of her effort, and the friction and heat the effort generated, the pooch would ice up in the bottom third, and the mustache, of course. When she was totally iced up, the boy let the snow and ice covered dog back into the house and went back to his snow shoveling duties. He snickered as he heard the muffled barks and yells as his mom chased the thawing dog throughout the house.

"Penny, ca'mere!" Penny, get on the rug, you're getting the house all wet! My rugs....!"

Around noon, he reached the front steps of Mrs. Lubely's house. She could now walk unobstructed and safe down the front walk.

"Come in and warm up," she said as she pushed the front door open.

He smiled at the old lady, brushed the snow off his parka and headed for the front door.

"Do you have a broom I can use, Mrs. Lubely?

"Why sure, come in."

"Let me use the broom to brush the snow off my boots so I don't track up your rugs," he said. He was well mannered even though he had thoroughly enjoyed setting a thawing dog loose on his mother's rugs.

"Maybe you can just slip out of them and we'll put them on this little rug just inside of the door. Would that be all right?" she asked.

"That would be fine, Mrs. Lubely."

He went inside the small wooden house and stepped on the rug where he unbuckled his overshoes and took off his parka. She handed him a towel to wipe his face, hands and hair.

"Have some cake and hot chocolate," she said to him as she leaned against her cane and motioned for him to sit on the couch. The hot chocolate had a marshmellow floating and melting in it. The cake sat tall, layered with chocolate frosting, on one of her good china plates. One of her best silver folks lay on a freshly laundered cloth napkin. Even though he was only a boy, in this home, he would be treated as any honored guest. She didn't know the meaning of everyday wear and paper napkins.

"Oh, that looks great," the boy said as he went to the couch and sat down. "Thank you Mrs. Lubely."

"It's the least I can do for all of the work you do for me."

She reached out for the arm on her chair but may have misjudged slightly as she started to stumble. The boy jumped from the couch to steady her.

"Are you all right Mrs. Lubely?"

"Oh yes," she said. "I wasn't paying proper attention. Finish you little snack. I am just fine."

As the boy got up to leave, she picked up the five-dollar bill and followed him to the door where she put it in his coat pocket.

"You buy something nice for yourself," she said as she patted the pocket.

"Oh, I can't take that Mrs. Lubely.

"Well I want you to have it just the same."

"Well thank you and thank you for the hot chocolate and the cake. It was really good."

"You're welcome," she said as she held her front door open as the boy left the house.

"Bye, Mrs. Lubely," the boy said as he turned toward the snowy front yard. He still had some cleaning to do on her walk but he was done for the day unless the wind or the state snowplow decided to rearrange things.

"Did you get Mrs. Lubely's walks done?" she asked her son as he walked in the door. He laughed as he saw the damp dog penned up in the corner by a stack of clothing baskets. "Don't let the dog out of there until she is dry," his mom ordered. "Did you see Mrs. Lubely?"

"Yup," the boy said. "She gave me five bucks."

"You don't need to be paid to do her walks."

"She insisted, Mom. Plus, she was lucky I was there, she almost fell."

"She fell?" his mom said as she wheeled around to verify what the boy was saying.

"I caught her."

"Was she outside?"

"No. Her living room."

"What were you doing in her living room?"

"She made cake and hot chocolate for me."

"You didn't make her trip or anything did you? She isn't very steady even with that cane."

"No Mom, I didn't make her trip. She was reaching for a chair and misjudged the distance I think."

"Oh the poor soul, her eyesight is really getting bad. I am going to call and make sure she is OK." She turned and walked to her telephone stand and sat down. She picked up the receiver and said, "Francis, give me Anna Lubely, Please."

'Hello Anna? This is Bun. Are you OK? I heard you almost fell."

"Well that's what he said but I just wanted to check and be sure you were OK."

"Are you sure? I can call and take you to the doctor if you don't feel well."

"Oh. Ok. But you call if you need anything, please."

"Ok. Oh yes, I'll still come for tea at three. Oh Sister will be there? How nice. I will see you then. Bye."

"She's fine," she said to her son. "I am going over there this afternoon at three and have tea with her and the big nun."

"The one that wears that black outfit and looks like a big black table-cloth blowing on the line when she comes down the street?'

"That's her," but she is very nice.

It was hard for Mrs. Lubely to bend over and look in her oven to check on her prize baking. Marcia sent her some nice tart Granny Smith apples and she turned them into a prize pie, a perfect treat for her afternoon guests. She learned against her cane as she opened the oven door, pulled on the shelf, and slid the masterpiece pie out of the over. She clutched the cane close to her side, reached for the other hot pad, and gently picked up the pie and slowly brought it up to the counter top and the waiting hotplate. It seemed like minutes instead of seconds as she balanced the pie and herself and leveraged the pie to the counter.

She looked at her hands. They were once as white and soft as fresh cream with a hint of pink. Now they were nothing more than thinly covered bones, the knuckles ravaged by arthritis. The brown spots of age had stolen her youth but not her dignity. She was still the gracious lady. It just took more concentration and more time to prepare a memory for her guests.

"Come in Bun," she said as she opened the door for her good neighbor.

"Oh your house always smells so nice, Anna."

"I put a cinnamon stick and some cloves into a hot apple cider."

"Oh that's what it is."

"Well look who is right behind you Bun."

Her neighbor turned just in time to she the big nun in her black habit doing battle with the wind.

"Hello, hello," the nun said as she came up the step with open arms. "Bless you good neighbor Bun," the nun said as she gave Bun a hug, "and just look our perfect China doll," she said as she gently put her hands on Mrs. Lubely's face and kissed her on the forehead.

"Come in, come in," Mrs. Lubely said as she leaned on her cane and held the door for her two friends as they came in out of the cold.

"Look at you," the nun said. "Perfect white hair. Perfect nails. Perfect jewelry with brooch on her coat lapel. Why if I weren't sworn to simplicity, I would be jealous. Aren't you jealous, Bun?"

"Why no, Sister," Bun said. "Envious but never jealous. Jealous is a Lutheran sin, don't you know." The nun howled at the friend joust.

"Please sit down," Mrs. Lubely said as she motioned to her couch and matching Queen Ann chairs.

"You have such beautiful things, Anna," the nun said as she took her seat on the couch. "They show a lifetime of love."

"And memories," chimed in the neighbor.

"To be sure," the nun said.

"How is your son?" the nun asked. "George isn't it?"

"Why he is just fine and his family is fine she said as she beamed from the question." She turned and took a picture from the end table. "This is George and his family. They sent it to me for Christmas."

The nun took the picture and squinted. "What a lovely family," she said. "Very blessed."

"And all is well with you, Bun?"

"Oh fine. We're all fine."

"You should bring Anna to the convent for tea some afternoon. We would love to try and convert you," she said as she threw back her habit and head and chuckled.

"I've only just learned how to pray the Lutheran Rosary, Sister."

The nun howled with laughter and slapped her knee. "You must come some afternoon. I cannot deny the other sisters an afternoon of your company. Even Mother Superior might split a lip."

"OK, we'll come someday."

"Wonderful, oh Anna can I help?" the nun said as she saw her old friend trying to carry the hot teapot into the room.

"Yes I suppose you could. It's a little heavy for me with this cane and all."

"I know how perfect everything usually is here, but let's bend the rules a little today," the nun said as she took the teapot and helped the old lady to her chair.

"Here we go," the nun said as she poured the tea in each of the three cups on the silver tray. Maybe we should call Lenyce and make sure this gets in the Cedar County News that I poured, " she said as she laughed.

"You would be the toast of the town, Sister," Bun said.

"Is that apple pie I smell?" the nun asked as she headed back to the kitchen with the teapot. "Why it is! And here are three plates ready for a nice warm slice."

The nun cut the pie and brought the plates to the living room. "What else?" she asked. "Oh a prayer." She reached out for a hand from each of the two ladies.

"Blessed Mother hear our prayer on this beautiful snowy day that we may always cherish the friendships you give us, that kindness becomes the warm tea of our hearts, and that love holds us together like a warm apple pie. Thank you for good neighbors, even though they be Lutheran and good fiends. In the name of the Father, Son and Holy Spirit, Amen."

They chatted and laughed and sipped tea and ate pie. By nightfall, a new prayer card lay on the kitchen table, the China was washed and put away, and a pie with four pieces missing, sat under a cover of waxed paper. Nothing but the sound of the tick-tock of the mantle clock could be heard in the house except for the bedside prayer of a little old lady who was grateful for another day of life.

It's Still
a Good Car

◆

Her brothers and sisters were all gone. Some of her closest friends were gone. That is often the price for living a long life and she was closing in on her eighty-fourth year. Her life was simple now and she filled it with as much activity as she could stand. She still had daily pain in her back from spinal problems caused by osteoporosis. She started her day with a heavy dose of prescribed medication for high blood pressure, and special vitamins.

She had daily routine. The Omaha World Herald® came by seven. She always read the sports section first. She had coffee made by eight. She was showered and in her chair by the window reading the paper by nine. She watched as her new friends, mostly young, drove off to work. They waved at the "tin house" even thought they couldn't see her for sure. They knew she was there by the window. She always was.

The trailer court brought her a new mix of friends. They were older and retired or young and just getting started with their lives. Trailer living gave both groups the best of something to call home. The trailers were simple, inexpensive, sometimes quiet, and always easy to maintain. It was a new neighborhood for her where the neighbors were all snuggled tightly together and everyone knew each other's business.

By ten, one of her older neighbors from just across the street was at the front door. He always came for coffee and took a few minutes to visit about current events in the town.

"What's new with you today?" she asked.

"Damn cat was walking on my car during the night," he said as he pulled off his baseball cap and entered the trailer. "Them people who own cats should keep them in at night or put them on a leash."

She knew better than to add anything to his statement. It would only make him madder than he already was. Cat tracks on his car and wild parties were two things he couldn't seem to tolerate in the trailer park.

"Them Spaulding brothers were a partying last night again," he said as he sat down in one of her rocking chairs. "Kept us awake until almost midnight."

"I didn't hear a thing," she said as she poured a cup of coffee and cut a slice of coffeecake for him. "I slept like a log but I have had kind of an itch on my arms."

"Oh?" he said as he leaned forward to take the coffee cup and slice of coffeecake. "Are you going to see Doc about it?"

"If it doesn't clear up, I will," she said as she sat down in her chair. "I don't think it is anything."

"Well if that middle son of yours finds out, he'll be up here in no time so you better go."

"I'll see what it is like in the morning and maybe get an appointment," she said. "What are you guys going to do today?"

"Well I have to be a pallbury this afternoon for Lawrence Schmidt."

"Oh, that's right," she said. "You worked together at the lumber yard didn't you."

"Almost thirty years. He was a real good fella. Nice family, too."

"Is Doris going with you?" she asked.

"No," he said.

"Isn't she feeling well?" she asked.

"She's kinda tired for all that goings-on next door last night," he said as he took his last bite of coffeecake and last swigs of coffee. "Well," he said as he pushed himself out of the chair, "guess I better be a going."

"You tell Doris hello for me and I will stop and see her this afternoon," she said as she walked him toward the door. "And don't be too hard on those boys, they are nice boys and just having a little fun, that's all."

"You wouldn't be so charitable if they had kept you up all night."

"What's a little lost sleep," she said. "I am glad they are close by and nice boys."

She enjoyed the liveliness and friendship of her younger neighbors and never wanted to be the old lady who complained all of the time. Her door was always open and she proudly wore the welcome mat in her heart.

On a good sunny day, she was off to the post office to get her mail. She liked to make that morning trip because it gave her time to have a look around and maybe exchange a few friendly waves along the route.

She drove a big older Thunderbird®. When she was behind the wheel, with the seat all the way forward, she could just barely see over the dash. She never went far from home. Her morning trip to the post office and perhaps a stop at the grocery store were her limit, except for Ladies Day at the country club and bridge club. In the winter, her neighbor got here mail and the grocery store delivered what she needed. Her mail was usually nothing more than junk mail and the weekly copy of The Cedar County News. Her boys didn't write her. They called and she was always close to her phone because each boy called at a specific time each weekend.

"You aren't walking on the ice and snow are you? Have you seen the doctor about your cold? Is the furnace working OK? How about your car—you're not driving on the ice are you?" She asked her questions, too.

"Are you eating enough vegetables? How are the kids? What are they doing? Are you drinking plenty of orange juice? Do you have any new accounts? When are you coming home to visit?"

This day was extra special for her. "I am driving up there this afternoon," her middle son said.

"Oh?" she asked. "Is something wrong?"

"Nope," he said. "I'll be there around two."

"Wonderful, I'll make some pork chops."

"Don't fix anything special, Mom," he said, "I am only staying a little while."

"Can't you stay the night?" she asked.

"No, he said. "I need to get back to Lincoln."

"OK honey, I will see you this afternoon."

She had lots to do in the couple of hours before he would arrive. Even though he said he didn't want anything to eat, she had other plans.

She dialed the wall-mounted phone and sat down at her small dining room table.

"People's Store, this is Marcia."

"Oh Marcia," she said. "This is Bun. Have the deliveries left yet?"

"Hi Bun, no I can still put an order on for you."

"Oh good, can you pick out three nice pork chops, a Betty Crocker® chocolate cake mix, a jar of applesauce, and a half gallon of milk for me?"

"Why sure Bun. Do you want the 2% or whole milk?"

"2% please."

"OK. I'll put it on the delivery truck for you."

"Thank you, Marcia."

It wasn't long before there was a knock at her back door and a boy from the Peoples Store handed her the brown sack with the bill stapled to the top of it.

"Oh thank you," she said to the boy as he dashed off to his running truck waving goodbye as he went. She went to her kitchen, and before long, her house smelled of chocolate cake and baked pork chops covered in gravy—his favorites.

She sat back in her chair by the window and waited for him to come. She switched the remote to a local channel which gave information about the community, including deaths in the area. Her neighbor walked out to his truck, dressed in blue suit and white shirt. "Pallbury," she said as she laughed about his misuse of the word.

She turned the channel to her favorite soap opera. There was nothing to do but sit, wait, and let the oven bake.

"Hey," he said as he stood in front of her chair. She had fallen asleep and didn't hear him come in.

"Oh, hi honey," she said as she woke from her sleep to see her middle son standing in front of her.

"Come outside," he said as he walked to the front door, opened it and waited for her.

"What's out there?" she asked.

"Come see."

"You got a new car, honey," she said as she pushed herself up from her chair and walked toward the font door.

"Close," he said.

He pushed the front door open so she could walk through. Parked behind the old Thunderbird® was a new mid-size little Mercury® four door sedan.

"Oh, you did get a new car."

"No, you have a new car," he said. "The old Thunderbird® is too hard for you to drive and I think you'll love this car. Come on, let's go for a drive."

"Oh honey, I can't take this car. You need a good car," she said as tears started to form in the corners of her eyes. "I don't deserve a good car like this. You keep it. I'll be fine with the Thunderbird®. It's still a good car."

"Well, that's too bad because I have already bought it and the only way I can take it back is if you can't drive it," he said as he opened the driver's side door and motioned for her to get in.

"How do these seat belts work?" she asked with great curiosity as she looked at the seat belt sticking out from the windshield support in front of her.

"They come down automatically when you turn the key," he told her. "Everything is electric so you won't have to wrestle with things. Here, put your fingers down here in front of the seat and we'll adjust it."

He gently took her aging hand and helped her work the seat controls. Full forward and full up and she was in a good position to see over the wheel and drive the car.

Once belted in place and ready to go, mom and son were off. They drove around the little town and waved. They drove around the park and made wide turns, practiced parking and backing up, and of course, sudden stops. The lesson went well.

"You seem to be able to handle this car just fine, Mom," he said. "Still want me to take it back?"

She smiled at him. "I love my new little car." She could see and handle driving again and that meant freedom which was more important to him than anything. He could handle the old Thunderbird®. It was still a good car and he didn't need much of a car anyway.

By nightfall, he was on his way back to Lincoln with the old Thunderbird®. The little blue Mercury®, freshly washed, sat in her carport for all to see. Over the next few weeks, he called not only at his usual Saturday time but also during the week to see how she was getting along with her new car.

"Are you driving your new car?" he asked.

"Why yes," she said. "I drove to bridge club. I drove to the country club. I drove to Coleridge. I've been out in the country and I've read the owner's manual a couple of times," she said with a heightened level of excitement, "and I passed my driver's test."

She found more freedom and nothing could have made him more happy. He wanted quality living for his mom. He wanted freedom for her. Those were the age fighters.

"But honey," she said as she paused, there was a serious note of worry in her voice, "there is something I need to tell you."

"What's wrong?" he asked. "Have you had an accident with your car? Are you OK?"

"No." She said in a quivering voice. "I had a CAT scan in Yankton today."

"A CAT scan? Why? What's wrong Mom?"

"Now I don't want you to worry," she said as she tried to calm his building fears. "I've had a terrible itch and the doctor noticed some jaundice around my eyes. He wanted me to have a CAT scan and he'll know more on Monday."

"Did he tell you what he is looking for? Why did he order the CAT scan? Do you want me to come up on Monday and go with you to the doctor?"

He was worried. He sat in his office chair fidgeting with worry and at the same time, trying to send a good strong, don't worry message through a phone that was shaking in his hand.

"No, honey," she said in a soft worried voice, "I'll call you when I get home from the doctor. Don't worry honey. Everything will be fine."

He didn't hear her words of comfort as his mind filled with worry throughout the entire weekend. She had told him to expect the call around noon on Monday. It was impossible for him to keep his mind on his work so he canceled his entire schedule for the Monday. She was faced with threat and he knew it was serious. She never wanted to burden her sons with medical worries. That didn't make any difference to him. Every time he called her, he carefully listened to her voice and her words for signs of problems. When he heard a cough or some congestion, he demanded to know if she had seen the doctor and if not, why not. This time he honored her wish even though he had filled his car with gas, canceled all of his appointments, and had a packed bag waiting by his front door. Finally the call came.

"Honey," she said, "the doctor called. They have found something. The hospital people are not sure what it is but Doc thinks it may be cancer."

His heart sank to his feet as he continued to listen. "I'll be there in a couple of hours," he said in his calmest voice.

"OK honey," she said as she started to cry. "The doctor is scheduling an appointment for me in Omaha. I'll know more by the time you get here."

He grabbed his overnight bag and headed for the Thunderbird®. He was about three hours from her in miles but sitting next to her in thought. His mind told him hope was what he must focus on but family history reminded him of the toll that cancer had taken from them. No one ever survived it. Cure rates meant nothing. Cancer came to this family to kill and now it had gripped his mom and a worried son was no match for it. He was more worried then he had ever been in his life.

He could think of nothing other than the threat of the killer inside of her as he threaded his way through an assortment of small country towns and farms as he drove the two-lane highway to Hartington. Finally, he was there. His first stop was the Doctor's office.

"Hi. I'm Bun's son," he said as he grabbed the ledge below the small window overlooking the receptionist. "If the doctor has a minute, I would like to talk to him."

He trusted this country doctor. After a few long minutes of waiting, he was sitting across from the doctor.

"The CAT scan indicates something by your mother's pancreas and intestine," he said with his calm and always thorough voice. "It's not exactly clear what it is but it is a mass of some kind."

"Is it cancer?"

"We can't be sure at this point so I have arranged for her to go to Omaha so they can do a procedure on Wednesday. They'll run a small television camera down there and have a look. If it is a gallstone, they'll take care of it on the spot and that should be the end of it. If it something else, the results will be evaluated by a surgeon I've recommended. He's one of the best in the country."

"What do you think it is?"

"I think it could be a growth," he said with his usual honesty. "It's in an unusual position for a stone and the scan didn't suggest a solid mass like a stone usually appears. She's in excellent health otherwise so we may have gotten a good early warning."

He knew he had an important two-part job in front of him as he left the doctor's office. There were arrangements to make and maybe more important, worry to abate.

She was sitting in her favorite chair, in front of her bay window when he came through the back door of the trailer. She looked at him and started to slowly bounce in her chair—a sure sign of tears.

"I've talked to the doctor," he said as he gave her a long hug and a forehead kiss. "We have to be in Omaha tomorrow so you can be seen at the hospital on Wednesday. I'll take you to Omaha in the morning."

"We're not going tonight?" she asked as she held on to his forearms.

"No," he answered. "I have to pick up the films and test results from the doctor in the morning and then we'll go."

"Oh, then I'll have time to get my hair fixed," she said as she tossed her hands up in the air in her usual way of dealing with an urgent problem. "I'll call and see if they can work me in first thing."

The small town news network was in full gear and within minutes, the phone started to ring with calls of worry and concern. Was it cancer? Would she have surgery? Was she going to Yankton, Sioux City, or Omaha? Was anybody there? Where was she going to stay? Would someone please call them when there was any news? Is there anything they could do? Was someone going to watch the trailer? Was someone going to get her mail? And of course, "Don't worry, we'll all be praying for you."

By noon the following day, they were in Omaha. The first procedure was high tech television.

"I am going to run a micro television camera, down her throat, through her stomach, and into the intestine where the common bile duct is located. We should be able to get pictures of the mass and be able to tell, almost instantly, what it is and what option we have," the doctor explained. "If the mass is a gall stone, the little camera is equipped with a laser which I can use to cut the stone apart and the problem would be solved. I will know more once we have completed the examination part of the procedure," he said as he turned and went back inside of the surgery suites.

"It wasn't long before he returned. "The news is not good," he said. "We found a tumor and it is malignant."

"This is the common bile duct and this is the tumor," he said as he used his pen and pointed out the items on a Polaroid® photo of the area. "As you can see, when we cut through it, the bile was released. That backed up bile is what caused her itching so relieving it should give her some relief from the itching problem" he continued. As you can see, the bloody nature of the mass strongly suggests a malignancy. There is no doubt in my mind that it is a malignant tumor."

"We would like to perform a surgical procedure as soon as possible," he continued as he put the photos back in the file and reached for a large color diagram of the affected anatomy. "The procedure we plan to do is called a Whipple procedure and what we'll have to do is remove the tumor, the gall bladder, a portion of her stomach, a portion of the pancreas, and a portion of the small intestine. It is major surgery but I believe she is in good enough health to tolerate it. I would like to do the procedure on Friday morning."

He sat in stunned silence. Malignant tumor. Major surgery. "Are there any other alternatives?" he asked.

"The only other option is to install a shunt, or a drainage tube around the affected area," he said as. "That will give her some relief from the itching but it is no cure. Eventually the tumor will spread to the pancreas and that will kill her."

"The Whipple procedure can cure her and you can expect another five or so years of good quality life," he explained. "There really isn't any other alternative. There will be no quality without it."

"Are you asking me to make the decision?" he asked the doctor.

"Yes," he said. "We'll need to schedule her soon."

"It's not my decision to make."

"Didn't she indicate that on the forms?" the doctor said as he flipped through the chart. "I thought she had decided that."

"I can't decide that for her," he said. "She'll have to decide."

"There really is no quality choice, here," the doctor said.

"Yes there is," he said almost in anger. "She has a choice. We'll wait until she has had time to consider the options. It's her choice and she'll make it. It's her life for God's sake."

"OK, we'll hold off," the doctor said as he closed the file. "She will be out of recovery shortly." He smiled and walked away.

She only had one day to consider her options. A resident was first to arrive on Thursday morning to answer her questions. The young resident's grandfather had undergone the Whipple procedure and had enjoyed another five years of high quality life. He had a long painful recovery which took about six months, but long term, he had good remaining years. She explained the other procedure to her, too.

"What should I do, honey?" she asked him as he stood close to her bed.

"I can't answer that question, Mom," he said. "We'll just have to ask a lot of questions and then you'll have to decide from what you hear."

"Honey, I've had a good life," she said as she looked up at him from the hospital bed. "I don't know if I want to go through all of this surgery."

"Is there someone else you want to talk to about it?" he asked.

"I'd like to talk to my doctor," she answered.

He pulled his cellular phone out of his jeans pocket and dialed the number to reach her home town doctor. He carefully explained, as best he could in layman's language, what the surgeon told them and handed the phone to his mother.

"Hi Doc," she said. He could tell she was worried and tired. "What do you think of all of this—should I have this surgery?"

"I can't make that decision for you," he said. "But, if it were my mother, which you have often been through the years, I would consul you to have the operation."

"Then I'll do it," she said.

The procedure was set for 11:00 Friday morning. It would be a two stage operation. Stage one was to locate the tumor, examine the surrounding the tissues to make sure it had not spread. If it had spread, the Whipple procedure would not be performed, and the shunt would be inserted. If the tumor had not spread, it would be removed and the Whipple procedure would be performed. Total time in surgery would be between two to seven hours.

Her recovery would start in Intensive Care. She would spend three to four days there before she would be moved to acute care for approximately ten days, and then she would be moved to a special unit, much like a nursing home, called restorative care, and if all went well, she could then go home. It would be a long, slow, and painful recovery for her.

"It went fine," the surgeon said as he came through the door of the third floor surgery waiting room and sat down across from the worried son.

"I'm sure she's cured," he continued. "She'll be coming out of recovery and will be moved to Intensive Care in about another hour or so. She withstood it wonderfully. I would say she has another good five years."

Five more Christmas seasons. Five more batches of mint cookies. Five more birthdays. Five more years of good small town living. His prayers and the prayers of a small town were answered.

"She won't be conscious this evening and will be on assisted breathing so you may as well go home and get some rest tonight," he continued. "She should be conscious early tomorrow morning."

As he waited in the chair-lined room, with a television blaring away with game shows and soap operas, his worry was changed to optimism. "Cured," he said to himself as he smiled. He went to the coffee machine and bought another cup of coffee. Finally the receptionist came over to him.

"Your mother is in Intensive Care," she said. "You can go in for just a few minutes if you would like."

He got up and went with her. "You'll have to push this button to gain entry," she explained.

The nurses hovered around the bed. The ventilator pumped in the air with steady twelve breaths per minute rhythm. The flexible, round blue tube ran from the small suitcase size machine to her face and was secured in the corner of her mouth by several bands of white medical tape wrapped around her head. A white piece of tape secured another device, which had a small red light, to her nose.

"That measures the oxygen content of her blood," the nurse explained. "That's what the numbers on that machine represent."

Another machine was measuring her heart rate, steady at eighty-two beats per minute, and her blood pressure, 156 over 94. Other machines were being attached to automatically administer morphine, antibiotics, and feeding. Tubes came out from under the sheets to drain urine. Other tubes came out of her nose. Two large canisters were starting to slowly fill with blood. Other bags of clear liquids, with long names and specific jobs, started there drips through a maze of clear plastic tubes to a busy intersections of plastic valves and into the IV's. The soft pink skin of her hands and arms were bruised like a prizefighter that had battled for twenty rounds. Her body was motionless except for the slight turns of her head as the ventilator took on the job of breathing for her.

"This was her first surgery," he told the nurse. She could see he was worried and anxious.

"She is doing very well."

"She is?"

"Oh yes, this is major surgery and her vital signs are all very good."

He looked at the lights, the tubes, and listened to the sounds. This was the first time he had ever seen her threatened and he was powerless to help her. There was nothing to do but wait.

"Are you going to stay here or are you going home?" the nurse asked.

"I think I'll go home tonight and gather up some things and come back tomorrow morning," he said as he tried to filter through his thoughts and come up with some kind of plan. "Will she be OK tonight?

"She'll be fine," the nurse said. "She won't wake up until morning I don't think."

"Then I will go now," he said. "Thanks."

He had a fifty-two mile drive to his home in Lincoln—most of it on Interstate 80—so he was back in his small Lincoln apartment in about an hour. He was tired. The fatigue and worry were taking its toll on him. He trusted what the doctor had told him and what he had seen. He decided a good night's sleep in his own bed would be best.

"Your mother is back in surgery," said the voice on the other end of the 2:30 a.m. phone call. "She's losing blood. She may have an artery that may have been nicked during surgery."

Within minutes, he was back on Interstate 80—aiming the car through the dark Nebraska night. Was he dreaming about the call he wondered? Was she really back in surgery?

"Hold on Mom," he softly sobbed as he struggled to stay sharp. "Hold on, I'm coming, Mom. Hold on. Please God, hold on."

"Excuse me sir, where are you going?" asked the armed hospital security officer as he bolted through the emergency room door and took dead aim at the door which lead to the Intensive Care area.

"My Mom is back in surgery," he said. "Get out of my damn way!"

"OK, OK, just be calm for a minute," the guard said, "I'll get you in there."

"She is still in surgery," the guard said as he hung up the phone. "The doctor knows you are here and will stop in the waiting room when they are done."

He took a seat in the empty waiting room and drank free coffee from a machine provided by the hospital. It was the same coffee he had drunk in hundred of airports—hot yes, tasteful, no. He needed sleep but he couldn't. Finally, at five in the morning, the now familiar doctor dressed in green from head to toe came through the door.

"We think we have the bleeding stopped," he started as he pushed the green surgical hat off the top of his short black and gray curly hair. "It wasn't what we thought it would be."

"What do you mean?"

"Well, we thought it might be an artery causing the bleeding, or the pancreas but it wasn't either," he explained as he sat in a chair across from the tired and worried son. "I used another procedure on the pancreas, which was actually pioneered by my brother," the doctor explained. "That seemed to stop the bleeding we could see around the pancreas but the problem seems to be one of weeping."

"Weeping? What do you mean weeping?"

"In older patients such as your mother, the organs tend to recover more slowly and 'weep' blood rather than bleed like say, from an incision. It is just a complication of her age."

"Are there any other complications that concern you?"

"I'm worried about infection," he continued. "Infection is always a possibility with this type of surgery and we'll have to watch very carefully."

"Can you control infection?"

"Yes," he said. "We have a variety of antibiotics available to us. For now, she's going to be fine. You should be able to see her in about an hour or so."

By noon she was starting to wake. The ventilator was doing her breathing and there was steady progress on all of the other monitors. Within two days, the ventilator was gone and replaced with oxygen treatments. She was alert enough to say "Oh!" several times an hour to underscore the pain associated with her surgical ordeal. Flowers filled the counter of Intensive Care and a stack of cards started to grow. Finally, she was moved to acute care.

"Do you know who I am?" he asked as he got close to her face. She couldn't wear her glasses because of the tubes in her nose and it was difficult for her to talk because she didn't have her teeth in place. Her mouth was terribly dry. She looked at his face and he watched as her eyes tried to focus. She pushed her swollen tongue slowly to the front of her mouth.

"My baby," she said slowly.

He smiled and gently brushed her gray hair with his hand. He leaned over and gave her a gentle kiss on the forehead. His mom was going to be OK.

As the days went by, she complained little except for pain when she was moved. She was still very weak and could only travel a couple of steps from her bed.

"Honey," she said as she held on to his arm for support, "I feel so weak and hungry, I could eat the hind end out of a skunk."

The surgeon watched as he helped her back to bed.

"Could I speak with you a minute," he said.

"Sure," he said as he pulled the sheet back over his mother.

"I'm concerned about he drainage and her pain level. We could have an abscess problem."

"What does that mean?" he asked. "Not more surgery I hope."

"I'm afraid so," the surgeon said as he put the metal chart against his chest and started to rub his chin. "I will have to go in an drain that abscess if she is going to start making progress."

"Oh God," he said. "She won't want to go through it again."

"This is a fairly simple procedure," he said. "It won't take long. Would you like me to explain it to her?"

"Yes."

The doctor turned and walked back into the room. He put the chart on the corner of her bed. She looked at him and instantly knew something was wrong.

"Oh no," she said. "Not again."

"I am afraid so," the doctor said, "but it is not a major procedure. We need to clean out a little area and we'll have you back in no time at all."

She started to cry and turned away from them.

"Mom," he said as he picked up her hand, and held it between his. "This isn't bad. It will help you recover more quickly so we can go home."

The next morning when he walked into her room, he saw the bed table which was used to hold lunch trays, covered with a green cloth and surgical instruments. There was a large pile of blood stained gauze in a special wastebasket. She was very uncomfortable and dopey from a morphine shot. Soon a nurse came into the room and started to clean up the remnants of the recently completed procedure.

"What happened?" he asked the nurse.

"I think the doctors took care of an abscess problem," she answered.

"In here! Why didn't he do it in the operating room?"

"The operating room is a sterile environment and this is an infection problem that really doesn't require surgery," she explained. "I'm sure it looks much worse than it is."

In two more days, she was moved to restorative care. She was inching closer to the time when she would be released. She was also becoming more of her old self.

"Give me some of that good coffee you get from that coffee stand downstairs."

Her took her for wheel chair rides and they ventured outside of the hospital so she could have a little taste of Nebraska spring air and sunshine.

"You remember the smell from the lilac bush by the corner of the old house?" she asked as she sniffed the spring air. "This place needs more lilac bushes."

He wasn't spending enough time with his business. He paid a heavy price to be with his mom but to him, that was a price worth paying. He was never more than minutes and a cellphone call away.

"Your mother collapsed this afternoon," the nurse said on the phone. "We have moved her back to Intensive Care."

"There is over a 53% spread in her bands which says she is producing a lot of immature white blood cells and they are being used as soon as they are being produced," the now frustrated surgeon explained. "I'll need to take her back into surgery because I believe she may have a narcoses of the bowel and if that bowel ruptures, it will probably be fatal."

"What is a narcoses of the bowel?" he asked.

"It's a dead section of bowel," the doctor explained. "It's essential that it be removed as soon as possible. I have asked surgery to schedule her within the next two hours."

"She is no longer conscious," the nurse said as she met him at the Intensive Care room door. "The doctor needs you to sign this consent form for surgery."

This time, he had to decide. Was there no other choice than more pain? Was this necessary? What would she want, he wondered? He didn't know. He signed the form.

"The bowel was fine. The original surgery is healing beautifully. We found a pocket of dried blood and removed it," the doctor explained as he once again sat across from him in the surgery waiting room. "I just don't know why she isn't responding better. We'll just have to wait and see."

"Why do you keep cutting on her?"

"I thought…"

"You thought that the last time, and the time before and you were wrong," he said. "That's my mother you're cutting up, God dammit. She's not an experiment. If you don't know, stop cutting."

"She'll be back in Intensive Care shortly," the surgeon said as he turned and walked away.

Once again, she was back in Intensive Care with a ventilator breathing for her and a larger assortment of bags with IV drips.

The next day, she was off the ventilator but she was fighting for air. She was barely conscious. Her vital signs were unstable. It was like a re-run without the hope they had before. This time, the doctors weren't sure why she wasn't responding.

"I'm going to have to put her back on the ventilator," the doctor said as they stood just outside the Intensive Care room. "She's having a hard time breathing and I'm worried about respiratory arrest."

"She could stop breathing and die?"

"Yes." The surgeon said. "She also has infection problems."

He went into the room and watched, as she gasped for each breath. He brushed back her hair and gave her a kiss on the forehead as he had done daily since the start. The respiratory therapist came in with the ventilator and asked him to step out of the room.

Her head was turned slightly to the right and the skin on her face was pulled tight by the tape that held the ventilator tube in place in the corner of her mouth. He bent over her and started to brush her hair when he noticed her left eye was covered in water.

"What did they do?" he said softly as he reached for a Kleenex®. "Did they put too much water on your forehead washcloth?"

He gently touched the tip of a Kleenex® tissue to the little pool of water, which had formed in the corner of her eye. He watched as it soaked up the water. He watched as her once soft gentle eye, now turned red from exhaustion and worry, tried to focus on him. Slowly, the eye started to fill with water again. He was startled and looked at her other eye. Both were fixed on his face, and from the corner of the other eye he could see a small stream of water running down her cheek and along the tape running around her head. He knew they were the tears of goodbye. The gentle twinkle he had loved so much slowly faded away as she entered a coma.

"It's OK to go Mom," he said as his tears joined her. "I'll be all right. Go be with Dad."

The light of her eyes slowly disappeared. He watched as the machines took over. He watched and listened for the machines to adjust to some kind of fighting signal from her body. There was nothing but the rhythm of machines as her life slipped slowly away. Seven days later he had the machines stopped and she passed away.

The cemetery plot was full now. The grass will soon cover the freshly disturbed brown earth and the drying early summer wind would soon wither a spray of fresh flowers and erase a message written on the fresh earth that simply said, "I love you."

The tin house will be the new home of some newly married couple, or maybe a teacher, or maybe a retired couple. In the back seat of the little blue Mercury® was her magic wand—the wooden spoon and the other cooking gadgets she used to change sugar and flour into Christmas and memories.

"Good bye Hartington," he said softly as he drove out of the trailer park and turned right on Highway 15. "Thanks for the love."

About the Author

$\blacklozenge$

Kenny Miller

Kenny Miller grew up in Hartington, Nebraska and it's clear this small Nebraska farm town had a big impact on his life. But like most small town kids, opportunity knocked in a bigger town.

His first stop after a University of Nebraska advertising education was Bridgeport, Connecticut. Kenny worked for Remington® Arms Company in sales promotion and advertising.

"Our advertising agency was a big New York firm so within the space of about five years, I went from a town of 1,500 peaceful souls to fighting that many people trying to get off a train at Grand Central Station.

The crowded New York life wasn't for him so he moved back to Nebraska and started an advertising agency.

One of his first clients was an aviation company and Kenny fell in love with flying. It wasn't long before this copywriter and commercial artist became a Learjet® co-pilot.

His flying days took him around the world with extended stays in Africa and the Philippines flying a camera-equipped mapping Learjet®. His flying career took an important turn when he was hired as one of country singer Willie Nelson's pilots.

"Willie is really responsible for this book," Kenny said. "One day, while we were waiting at the airport, I asked Willie how he created his hit songs. He told me when he got a song idea he wouldn't do anything with it right away, but if that idea was still rattling around in his head a few weeks later, he got busy. That's when I turned on my computer and started writing these stories.

Kenny is a marketing consultant who specializes in creating logos, taking on-site photography, and of course, writing business stories. His work has also appeared in *Private Pilot*® magazine.

"Writing allows me to listen to my heart," Kenny says. "The heart is also where forever lives."